Couples

Adventures at Hedonism II

By Jason Pinaster

ACKNOWLEDGMENTS

Cover credits: The background cover art was uploaded by Bcow to Flickr and is reproduced here pursuant to a Creative Commons licence. All photoshopping and cover design was done by me.

Acknowledgement: Many thanks for the suggestions from and proofreading by Sallyann Cole. All errors remain mine.

ISBN: 9781370053346
ISBN-13: 9781370053346

CONTENTS

Fiction: This story is a work of fiction. Names, characters, businesses, places, events and incidents are either the products of the author's imagination or used in a fictitious manner. Any resemblance to actual persons, living or dead, or actual events is purely and entirely coincidental and not intended by the author. In short: this story is not about you, anyone you know, or about the acts or omissions of anyone living or dead. This story is not about the model(s) photographed on the cover but represents a fictional fantasy created by Jason Pinaster. The amenities at Hedonism II are described as accurately as memories of several visits allow. The proposed artificial reef, the proposed development, the demonstration and the police response are complete fiction and exist only in my imagination. The fictionalized reef was private, without government authorization. However, there are several ongoing efforts to prevent shore erosion and to protect the underwater environment off Negril.

Couples: Adventures at Hedonism II

Chapter 1

Each time the Sandal's receptionist thanked the person at the other end of the line and hung up, the young couple's spirits sank another notch. They had arrived late at night at the upscale couples resort only to discover that their travel agent had made an error with their reservation and that the resort was fully booked. But their spirits rose each time the receptionist smiled at them, picked up his phone, and dialed again. They had long since given up trying to follow his rapid-fire Jamaican patois, but they tried to take encouragement from his smile. Outside, rain began to splash onto the pavement.

The young couple was the product of the global age: two Japanese accountants in their late twenties living in London, England. Keizo gave his wife a reassuring hug and she hugged him back. His five-foot-eleven frame was thin, almost delicate. He was holding his body upright, trying to be strong for his wife. She was even thinner than her husband, except where her feminine charms added graceful curves to her body. Their eyes were brown, their hair black—his short, hers long and flowing. Sweat was now showing through their elegantly tailored cream-colored linen vacation clothes.

Sandals, a luxury resort on Jamaica's west coast, was supposed to have been their reward for a year's hard work. Long lazy days sitting on the beach together. But now it looked like they might have to settle for a one-star room at the end of a two-hour bus ride back in Montego Bay.

The receptionist hung up and dialed again. Keizo looked around the lobby. Maybe there was somewhere they could rest for a few hours. But a squeeze from his wife's hand brought his attention back to the receptionist's conversation, "Yes, one couple." There was a pause. "One week." Another pause. "They have a credit card. Keizo and Yoshi Tomatsu."

The receptionist smiled at them. "I have found a room. At Hedonism. I hope that's alright?"

The young couple nodded in grateful unison. They had never heard of Hedonism. But a room, any room, would be a relief.

Then there was flurry of activity and the young couple found themselves, and their luggage, speeding away from the resort in a local taxi. The receptionist hadn't told them where they were going or anything about the resort, but there was apparently room at the inn and at this point in their travels, that was all Keizo and Yoshi needed to hear. Keizo felt his wife's head relax against his shoulder.

The taxi driver whisked them around a roundabout and opened his door for them. Keizo paid the driver and added a tip. A porter from the hotel lifted their luggage from the trunk and carried it up to the lobby. Keizo proffered a tip, but the porter waved it off.

A receptionist favored them with a welcoming smile. The marble counter in front of her made her look small, but the art deco polka dots on the wall behind her complimented the laughter on her lips.

"Do you have a room for us?" Keizo asked.

"Yah, Mahn, no problem," she nodded.

"Thank you so much."

The receptionist took their passports and credit card, then motioned to their right. "Why don't you see if there's still something to eat in the buffet?"

Yoshi suddenly realized that she was very hungry and pulled at her husband's hand. But he stood still. "Shouldn't we check in first?" Keizo asked, casting a glance at their luggage.

"Check in's no problem. You must be famished."

Famished was an understatement. They'd slept on the plane and missed dinner.

At this late hour, the restaurant was empty, the selection limited, but cold cuts, cheese, fruit pastries and soft ice cream had never tasted so good. The only other guests they saw were clustered around the bar at the end of the restaurant talking softly and watching the rain falling in the darkness.

Back in the lobby, the receptionist waved them over to a comfortable couch and returned their passports and credit card. "This will let you into the room," she said handing each a key card. She slipped an envelope into Yoshi's hand, "This explains the resort's amenities and theme nights."

The porter wheeled their bags to the room, leading them through the rain. By the time they'd arrived at their room, Keizo and Yoshi were thoroughly soaked.

The porter showed them where the bathroom was and how to operate the wall safe. He pointed to the sliding doors. "Dem go direct to the beach," he told them. Keizo proffered a tip but the porter shook his head, "No tipping at Hedo, mahn."

Yoshi watched her husband splash water onto his face. She was proud of how well he'd stood up during their long journey westward across the Atlantic Ocean. But she was especially proud of how he'd kept himself—and even her—calm throughout the ordeal of discovering their travel agent's error and the lengthy effort to find alternate accommodation. In all their years of being together—since they were sixteen, just finishing their lower level schooling—she had never been more pleased with her choice of mate.

Keiko watched his wife inspect their room as he toweled off his face. She peeked into the closet to his right, the king-sized bed in the middle of the room and the curtains at the far end. The rain had pasted her clothes to her skin accentuating the subtle curves of her breasts. She had never looked so sexy. Even the drowned-mouse look to her long black hair was beautiful. He chuckled at her embarrassment when she caught sight of herself in the mirror above the dresser. He couldn't wait until she saw the mirror that covered the ceiling above the bed.

His clothes looked even worse than hers. She motioned him out of the washroom and helped him out of his linen jacket. It was wet and clung to his body. She stumbled and they hugged. He was so hot—her furnace—and she felt warm for the first time in hours. She hung his jacket in the closet. When she turned back to him, he was holding his shirt out for her.

As she hung his shirt in the closet, Keiko could see the outline of his wife's panties through the back of her pants. He knew that they were black and sheer, but he had never seen them on her before. He had never touched her through the fabric. As soon as their plane had taken off, she had whispered into his ear, describing the new lingerie she was wearing underneath her linen pantsuit. He still remembered her giggles when he had had to adjust his hips.

Yoshi turned back to him. His face was lean, delicate, just a hint of angularity. Above his pants he was nude. He lacked even a wisp of hair—she liked him like that—so that she could see the soft outline of his physique without other distraction. It wasn't that he was muscular, a desk job saw to that, but still there were hints of muscle just beneath his smooth skin. She trailed her fingers down the center of his chest, glorying in how hard his ribs were, glorying in the softness of his stomach. When her hands reached his pants, she swiftly unbuckled them and pulled the zipper down. There was a bulge beginning to form under his briefs and she licked her lower lip.

Her fingers traced fire down his chest and into his belly. Below, he felt himself rising to meet her. But she merely pulled down his zipper, making no effort to touch him there. He knew she would want their wet clothes removed before she would be relaxed enough to embrace their passions. Sometimes her lack of spontaneity irked him, but tonight having to wait was turning him on. He quickly pulled his pants off and handed them to her, searching her face for any reaction to the bulge pressing outward against his white cotton underwear.

His hands helping her remove her rain soaked jacket were strong, yet infinitely gentle. Yoshi felt the jacket slide down the sleeves of her blouse with relief. As she turned around after placing her jacket on a hanger, he was right there, ready to hug her. She smiled, but motioned him back, and further back, and further back again. She caressed the top button of her blouse smiling at his rapt attention where her fingers touched the hard plastic. She undid the button, revealing only flat flesh beneath. She teased, then unfastened another.

He watched as her fingers popped the third button free, catching sight of the black outline of the top of her bra. The next button popping free revealed her skin under the sheer fabric of the bra. As always, the half-hidden skin was more alluring than nudity brazenly available to his eyes. Button after button came free, but she held her blouse together, revealing only the center of her bra and the cleavage where her breasts came together. However, when she reached the last button, she slowly pulled her blouse apart. Sheer black fabric perfectly cupped her breasts. Underneath, her dark nipples pressed forward, as if trying to poke through the lingerie.

Yoshi let him step forward then. Truth be told, she would have been disappointed had he been able to restrain himself further. She reached for his male member, both to hold him away from her and for the sheer joy of feeling his hard arousal. It was hot through the soaked cotton. When she pulled his briefs back, masculine musk and the scent of accumulated sweat mixed with the delicate aroma of rainwater to form an intoxicating cocktail in her nostrils. She pulled the briefs down a few inches and heard them plop against the floor.

As soon as he'd felt her release her grip on him, Keiko pushed her back against the wall. He fumbled with her zipper and she pretended to squirm but soon he had the zipper down and her pants pushed half way down her thighs. This awkward position forced her to remove her pants and turn to the closet to hang them up. The outline of her pelvis was on full display. Keiko pursued his advantage to inspect her sheer lingerie, to feel the smooth curve of her buttocks, the yearning in her nipples.

His concentration on his hands allowed Yoshi to escape around him, putting the bed between them. She cocked her hips to one side to allow him to admire her panties and pulled her shoulders back to emphasize her breasts. The admiration in his eyes warmed her with the security and excitement of being wanted. She admired him in return, his *inkei* jutting out like a sturdy flagpole up and out from its curly black forest, his paired *kintama* being pulled up and under.

She reached behind back to undo her bra. She knew he liked to be the one to undress her, especially to remove her lingerie, but she could see that he was aroused enough already. She dropped her bra to the bed and watched his eyes gravitate to her jiggling *oppai*, and especially to the hard little buttons in their centers. She pulled her panties down to reveal the dark black ringlets of her *inmo*, then pulled them back up and down to alternately hide and reveal her luxuriant curls. His desire radiated across the mattress, stoking heat in her core.

Keiko shot onto the bed and was half way across before she could react. Yoshi moved to her left but all that accomplished was to allow him to corner against the wall beside the head of the bed. She had meant to escape, but the cravings in her body had betrayed her. He gently pulled her down to the bed, her *oppai* jiggling as she fell. Then he was beside her, his hand caressing atop her panties, then slipping underneath to slide his fingers through her swirling *inmo* hair.

His touch was electric and Yoshi felt her hips drawn upward toward his graceful and precise fingers, up against the soft firmness of his palm. Inside she felt moisture gather within her *chitsu* and felt the moisture warm and boil. Outside, his fingers gently caressed the hard little knob of her *kuritorisu* and she knew that he must be feeling it hard and hot against his fingertips.

Beside him, his wife smelled of cherry blossoms after a light springtime rain, the warmth of her body releasing hints of lilac and vanilla with an elusive undercurrent of almond. Her *oppai* were flat, and properly deferential atop her chest, but her nipples jutted insolently upward. And when he touched her breasts, Yoshi gasped.

Keiko sensed his wife's fingers trace up his thighs then tickle the undersides of his *kintama,* tingling them. She turned toward him and gave his large eggs a gentle squeeze causing his *inkei* to sway back and forth with the intoxicating sensations. He marveled at the exactitude of her touch—just enough pressure for pleasure, but not so much as to propel him forward, always leaving the next stage to his initiative.

Yoshi struggled to maintain her focus on her fingers, on her stimulation of her husband. But her body was drawing her attention to the warmth of the awakening excitement within her pelvis and especially along her *chitsu.* She wrapped her fingers around his *inkei* and lightly stroked up and down his shaft. She was waiting for him to make the next move, but she hungered for him to be inside her, to be filling her, to be caressing her *kuritorisu* with his every thrust.

He stroked his fingers lightly up and down between her thighs and felt her quiver in response. He knew he should massage her softly, with long gentle motions. He knew that she required sustained stimulation before he should enter her. He knew that he should attend to her needs first. But her stroking fingers overwhelmed this knowledge and he pushed her fully onto her back then climbed atop her. He felt her legs spread beneath him as her smiling eyes welcomed him into her *chitsu.*

Yoshi felt her eyes flutter and she couldn't help but close them as she felt him push between her labia, felt him enter her, felt discomfort and joy accommodating his girth sliding within her. His pulling himself back out opened her eyes, joining their smiles. Every time he pumped himself in and out, she felt the warmth in her *chitsu* spread up her spine, into her buttocks, down her thighs.

Keiko knew that his wife required more lengthy thrustings that he to reach climax, but he was almost never able to last long enough for her. So ordinarily he'd come fast, then wait a few minutes for his *inkei* to recover. Afterwards, the second time, he'd come slow. But tonight, with their lengthy travels and the travails at Sandals, he wasn't sure he'd have the stamina to go again, so he replayed last week's soccer match over and over, doing his best not to notice how beautiful Yoshi was.

Every time he entered her, every time their curly hairs down below mashed together and intertwined, Yoshi fell in love with her husband. The feeling of falling in love was as sharp and powerful as it had been the first time: when he had, without complaint, bought her a second ice cream cone after she'd foolishly dropped the first one to the ground. But now the feeling was deeper, encompassing every kindness that had ever passed between them. Now the feeling burned with the prolonged passion of a happy marriage.

Yoshi was a devoted and worthy wife, but Keiko struggled mightily to maintain his focus on the battles for the ball at midfield, on strikers shooting, on the goalie blocking.

Yoshi felt the warmth moving up her spine start to fill her lungs, mixing the joy of the love in her heart with the ardor boiling below. She breathed in to maintain the balance, but when she exhaled, the heat inside her pelvis overpowered everything else and she abandoned herself to the driving fury of sex. She rocked her hips towards him, against him, demanding more and more and *more*!

Keiko concentrated on the goalie moving into position, on his readying to dart left or right depending on the motions of the striker. The striker moved left, the goalie moved right and Keiko could hold himself back no more.

Yoshi could feel Keiko beginning to come and she raced towards her own climax, desperate to reach it in time, desperate to reach it before his thrusts shuddered to a stop and he fell down to the bed beside her. She caught sight of his buttocks in the mirror above the bed, of his buttocks frenetically clenching and releasing in time with the thrusts she felt inside her *chitsu*, against her *kuritorisu*, atop her *oppai* and nipples, against her *whole* body. She became his clenching buttocks! And in that moment of union the universe exploded inside her *chitsu*!

Keiko exploded inside her, spurting his life force into Yoshi's fertile field, feeling the pumping at the base of his *inkei* and up its shaft, feeling the spasms releasing concentrated pleasure out the other direction, up his spine, down into his toes.

A wave thundered up her spine. Then nothing as above he trembled then jolted to a stop. She felt only warmth and held her breath. Then he moved again, but slowly and gently, and soft tingles trickled down her legs.

When Keizo and Yoshi awoke the next morning, they quickly dressed in bright tropical attire, his shorts long, hers shorter, and sandals. Yoshi did up the top button of her blouse and inspected herself in the mirror. They planned to walk along the beach on their way to breakfast.

Keiko slid the sliding doors open and stood aside to allow his wife to exit. He noticed the private Jacuzzi tub off to one side. The sky was blue, the air hot and humid, but not too humid. His wife stepped out. He put his foot in the doorway. The tub would be fun to relax in. Play footsies—

But Yoshi was pushing him back into the room. "Keiko!" she wailed, gesturing wildly outside. But before he could see what she was pointing at, she had pulled the curtain to cover the sliding doors.

"Yoshi! What—"

He moved to pull the curtain open, but her hand on his prevented him from touching it. "Don't!" she cried, her voice fluttering.

"Yoshi?"

She took a deep breath. "There are people outside."

He kissed her forehead. "It's not our own private beach. It's for the whole resort." He reached for the curtain."

"*Hadaka*!" she screamed.

"*Nu-do*?!?" She must be mistaken; there couldn't be nudists out their front door.

"*Ee!*" Yoshi confirmed, "*Supponpon!* Utterly naked bare assed!"

Keiko pulled the curtain open just a crack so that he could see outside. Yoshi was right. There were all manner of people on the beach. Some were walking by. Some were gathered in groups, talking, some were swimming. One couple was kissing passionately, putting on a show, though only a few were watching them. And everyone was stark raving nude!

Below him, he felt his wife open another crack in the curtains. On the beach, a large muscular man walked by followed by two women, one white, one black, walking close together. A couple in their mid-forties tried to strike up a conversation with the women, but the two ladies seemed to prefer their own company. Another couple, older, walked quickly by, his male member flopping from side-to-side. A somewhat rotund man, dark-skinned, but not black, helped his wife adjust herself on a beach chair. As the brown-skinned woman spread her legs, Keiko saw everything, even a flash of pink between the center of her thighs. He had to remember to breathe.

Keiko and Yoshi watched together for what seemed an eternity before their stomachs started to growl.

"Maybe we should go out the other door," Yoshi suggested.

He nodded and they walked to breakfast atop paved pathways instead of along the sand-covered beach. They glanced into the gym. She was relieved to see that everyone stretching and lifting weights was fully clothed.

Also, thankfully, everyone was clothed in the main dining area. Yoshi and Keiko piled their plates full of fresh pineapple, yogurt, salmon and toast, then found a secluded table in the corner.

"Interesting scenery," he began.

"I suppose you want me to take my clothes off," she countered.

"It could be exciting."

"We don't need to prance around."

"We don't *need* to do anything."

Yoshi nodded, filling her mouth with a bite of salmon, cream cheese and toast. He was right. But it might be exciting to go topless. The men she'd seen earlier, with their long john silvers dangling had been an eye opener. Before this morning, Keizo's *inkei* had been the only mature male sexual organ she'd ever seen. It might be interesting watching other men prance around. They filled their plates again and took their second course back to their room. Each propped open a laptop and began to Google "Hedonism II".

"There's a nude beach and a prude beach," she noted.

"And lots of swingers."

"Swingers?"

"Couples who have sex with each other," he explained, looking up.

"Keiko!"

He dove back into his laptop. "Watersports are included.

Snorkeling, kayak, even scuba."

"We don't know how to scuba."

"We should try new things. There are classes."

"Our life insurance will go up if we scuba," she reminded him.

"No scuba," he agreed. For accountants, the bottom line was determinative.

"There's a nightly show, and dancing," she noted.

He got up and clicked his tongue to a techno beat, moving his hips in time with his clicks. She divided her attention between her husband and a video of dancers rubbing against each other in the resort's disco.

Keiko finished with a John Travolta pose right out of *Saturday Night Fever*. She suppressed a chuckle and Googled "swingers".

Chapter 2

Christopher Lang, wearing denim cut-off shorts and a 'Save the Reef' T-shirt, strode into the lobby where he joined a steady stream of similarly clad guests. Chris was a handsome brown-skinned man in his mid-forties who identified as African-American. He exuded confidence up and down his six-foot-two-inch ramrod straight frame. Then again, it was easy to exude confidence with broad and muscular shoulders. His curly black hair was cut short. He stood behind a woman in line for the bus that would take them to the demonstration site. The woman in front of him looked vaguely familiar.

While he was waiting, a South-East Asian couple in bright tropical wear, approached him. "What is this 'save the reef'?" asked the rotund male.

"It's a protest against a development which is slated to occur on the proposed site of an artificial reef restoration project." Chris reached into his satchel and proffered two protest T-shirts to the couple. "Would you like to join in?"

She smiled back at him but shook her head. "Maybe later."

The line in front of Chris had moved ahead and the door to the bus was starting to close. He jumped aboard and slid into the seat by the driver.

The center of the demonstration was located by the front gate of the construction site for a new hotel. The occupants of Chris's bus joined the protestors who were walking in a circle in front of the gate. Each was carrying a sign accusing the developer of destroying ocean habitat. Behind the gate, several construction workers lounged on a set of crates. Off to one side was a small mound of snorkeling equipment. All the demonstrators were wearing "Save the Reef" T-shirts.

A perky Jamaican teenager handed each of the newcomers a small pamphlet. It explained that a private group had started to rejuvenate the local coral reef. They had constructed a series of mesh globes, each attached to runners, acquired purpose-built cinder blocks, fashioned specially-fabricated half-globes and placed all of these on the ocean floor. Upon each half-globe, donor coral colonies had been affixed and, in the years to come, would grow into mature coral. Or at least they would grow into mature coral if they weren't disturbed. The new developer's plan was to construct a concrete wharf out into the ocean. And the wharf was slated to go right through the center of the new coral colonies. The developer maintained that there was nowhere else to place the wharf.

As the others read the pamphlet, Chris watched another bus approach.

Keizo and Yoshi were among the new arrivals on the next shuttle bus. The young couple was wearing swim-suit bottoms and flip-flops. Yoshi's breasts jiggled under her 'Save the Reef' T-shirt. Off to one side, two policemen leaned lazily against a coconut tree.

There was a rumble in the distance. The rumble turned into a roar. Then the roar turned into a phalanx of bulldozers rounding the corner and heading straight for the demonstrators milling in front of the construction site gate.

Chris rallied the protesters to form into a triangle. He stood at the point of the human triangle, directly in front of the approaching bulldozers. Several of the women bared their breasts. The policemen roused themselves and signaled for the bulldozers to stop.

An argument ensued between the bulldozer drivers and the policemen. The police said they were there to keep the peace. The drivers said they had right of free passage on the highway. Diesel fumes wafted over the protesters. After a half-hour standoff, the bulldozers turned around and left and the police resumed their place by the tree.

The demonstrators jumped up and down in glee, shouting at the retreating construction equipment. Everybody hugged everybody else.

As the protesters were returning to their walking circle, Chris realized that he was hugging a white woman in her early forties, soft and hard in all the right places. She was half a foot shorter than him, lithe. Her brunette hair framed the face of a model complete with blue eyes and full lips.

"Diane?"

"Chris!"

Chris inspected the woman—Diane Chumak, his former lover— for any sign of age but could fine none. She was wearing an elegant beige yoga outfit which made her every movement seem feline. She was thin, but not without the definite curves of feminine sexuality. Her nipples were hard buttons under her sports bra. "You are a sight for sore eyes!" he told her.

"You too," she nodded as she inspected his six-pack abs. "Your body tells me that you're still in construction?"

He nodded. "Foreman."

She pointed at her bare ring-finger. "Divorced."

He raised his corresponding finger. It was also bare. Neither finger had a tan-line.

She hugged him again and he felt a frisson of arousal. "Why did I ever let you go?" she moaned wistfully.

"We both wanted different things."

"Unimportant things."

"Do you have children?"

She shook her head and held him tightly. "You?"

He gently pushed her back, looked into her eyes and shook his head. "No. No kids."

"I should have said yes to you. When you asked me."

He looked down at the gravel beneath his feet.

The silence between them started to hang heavily and she hurried to push it away. "Have you been back since, to Hedo?"

He nodded and looked up at her. "Once. With Charlene. But it wasn't her thing. You?"

She shook her head. He bent down and kissed her. She pushed herself up on her tiptoes to increase the passion of their joining. He felt sparks, then flame spreading along her lips. She smelled his musk, smoky in her nostrils. He felt her moan, deep in her chest. She felt a new muscle, strong and straight, press against her stomach. Suddenly there was applause all around them and they parted, flushed and happy, with only a hint of embarrassment.

Chris and Diane, holding hands, moved off to one side to continue their conversation. "Why'd you come down now?" he asked.

"I needed to recharge my batteries. Saving the reef and staying at Hedo seemed the perfect combination." She pointed to his T-shirt. "For you, I'm guessing it was all about the reef."

He shook his head. "All work and no play will send Chris to an early, not to mention boring, grave."

"Still chasing fantasies?"

He nodded.

"So what's your fantasy for this week?"

17

"I've always wanted a threesome. You?"

"I need to break free of my inhibitions. So, sex in public. Preferably in the sea."

"Doing the fertility dance in mother ocean sounds like a perfect battery-charger."

She squeezed his hand.

A black car with a claxon siren blaring careened around the curve and skidded to a stop, small puffs of dust rising from its tires. Two uniformed policemen exited. The driver held the back door open. Another police officer, clearly of higher rank, stepped from the car. The two policemen leaning against the tree immediately jumped to attention and marched over to the car. The demonstrators watched transfixed as all four junior officers stood at attention in front of their superior who barked out loud, but incomprehensible, orders.

The four officers took out their batons and marched towards the demonstrators. As they approached, they raised their batons, as if to strike.

"Disperse!" yelled Chris.

The demonstrators backed off in all directions and cleared a path for the officers.

Soon the four police officers had marched right into the center of the demonstrators. They looked confused. The superior officer shouted something.

"Strip and sit!" yelled Chris.

Everyone except the young Japanese couple removed all their clothes. Yoshi and Keizo removed their T-shirts. At least above the waist they were nude. Yoshi bounced her shoulders back and forth, jiggling her breasts suggestively at the officers. Everyone else sat down. One of the officers took a step towards Yoshi. Keizo pulled his wife down to the ground beside him.

"Save the fish!" shouted Chris. "Save the fish!"

Diane joined in and clapped her hands between each shouted slogan.

Then everyone joined in with chants of "Save the Fish" in unison followed by a loud clapping of the hands. "Save the fish!"

"The reef is illegal," shouted the superior police officer. The junior officers looked confused. Two older women stood and caressed the youngest of the officers, kissing him on the cheek. He pulled away. Other women stood.

The four officers retreated towards their car. They yelled and gestured at each other. Chants of "Save the fish!" prevented Chris from hearing what they were saying.

Finally the superior officer gestured towards the back door which the driver held open for him. He got in, followed by the two officers who had come with him. The remaining two officers watched the car drive away then returned to leaning lazily against the coconut tree.

The demonstrators jumped up and down and cheered. The women hugged; the men exchanged high-fives. There were continued rumblings of "Save the fish!", then hoots and hollers.

While some demonstrators put their clothes back on, Chris and Diane remained nude. The original couple from the Garden of Eden. Sweat accentuated his brown-skinned muscles. She admired how hard his muscles were, how free of fat was his waist. She marveled at the tight black curls atop his manhood. His brown eyes lingered on her lean but fully rounded breast and her pubic mound below. Memories of what lay within caused his penis to start to swell.

Diane pointed at the snorkeling equipment. "Why don't we go check out our progress under the water?"

He smiled and nodded as they donned swimming suits. At water's edge, they added fins and masks.

By the shore, the ocean bottom was rocky, bleached white, and devoid of life. Ten feet further out, there was some sea grass and a lone orange starfish. Twenty feet further out, a sign proclaiming the restoration project was bolted to a large stone. Little clumps of coral were beginning to grow. Sparkles of pigment replaced the white desert. Several large and colorful parrotfish swam by.

The artificial coral field was about fifty feet wide and extended out a further hundred yards in front of them. Chris and Diane swam half way down its length before the water turned deep. A barracuda swam parallel to them, watching curiously. A school of yellow grunts parted in front of them. Two leopard rays cavorted through the water. The green head of an eel poked out from his hole. A trio of cuttlefish turned iridescent, almost transparent, as they approached. When they swam lazily back to shore, the barracuda left.

Back on land, Chris and Dianne turned around to look in the direction of their swim. "Maybe later we'll scuba," he ventured.

Diane nodded. "Where we swam, that's right where they want to dump their concrete wharf."

"It should be dumped on their heads!"

As Chris and Diane returned to the demonstration site, a shuttle bus disgorged a new set of protesters, along with refreshments. Some of the demonstrators got on the bus to return to their resorts.

The new group included the South East Asian couple Chris had spoken to earlier that morning. They were still dressed in same outlandish attire. Chris strode up to them and extended his hand towards the rotund male. "Glad to see you came," he told him. "I'm Chris."

"I'm Bassim and this is my wife Damini." She was much more slender and slightly younger than her husband.

Damini eyed Chris up and down, obviously enjoying what she saw. Her red-lipsticked lips parted in a smile.

"Why are you demonstrating?" asked her husband.

Diane touched Bassim's red and blue and green and yellow shirt, adoring it colors. "We want to stop the developer from pouring concrete on the reef." She touched his belly and enjoyed its jelly jiggle. She looked down as Chris proffered an extra large Save-the-Reef T-shirt in his direction. "Would you like a T-shirt?" she asked, undoing his middle button.

Bassim nodded and quickly undid the rest of his buttons.

Diane turned to Damini and offered a smaller T-shirt to her. "And you?"

Damini nodded and quickly undid her shirt, making sure that both Diane and Chris caught a good look at her white lace bra.

Three white Jamaican police cars rounded the corner in the distance. Their sirens were flashing but their claxons were silent. Their superior's black sedan brought up the rear. Four uniformed officers clambered out of each of the white cars, two out of the black sedan. Another officer held the door open for his superior who shouted orders at the other officers.

Chris formed the demonstrators into a triangle facing the officers.

The fourteen officers formed a long line facing Chris and his triangle. They were holding onto a rope stretched out in front of them. Zip-ties dangled from the rope. The officers took two steps forward. A relentless, irresistible row. Three more steps and their rope would be pressed against Chris's torso.

"Save the reef," chanted the demonstrators.

Two large vans careened raucously around the corner. Their roofs were festooned with satellite dishes. When they skidded to a stop behind the black sedan, the logos of one local and one international news service were clearly visible. Camera crews and reporters gushed forth.

The police superior yelled at the reporters. The reporters yelled back. The superior gestured back towards the vans. The reporters gestured towards the demonstrators.

The line of police officers which had been approaching the demonstrators stopped and looked back towards the reporters, uncertain as to which group they should be corralling.

At length, the reporters took up positions on each side of the demonstrators, but far back from the impending confrontation. The line of police officers regrouped and took another step forward. One more step and the rope would be wrapped around Chris's belly.

"Nude!" shouts Chris. He and Dianne fling their swimsuits aside.

Almost everyone else flings their clothes aside as well. Bassim and Damini strip to their underwear. Damini hesitates a moment, then removes her bra. Her breasts have some sag in them but they point forward, proud, her nipples engorged into sharp points. The young Japanese couple goes fully nude, displaying pubic patches freshly-trimmed into narrow triangles pointing down. The line of fourteen police officers hesitates. The camera crews take a step forward. The reporters position themselves in front of the cameras and begin narrating a description of the unfolding events.

The superior police officer shouts an order and the long straight line of officers begins to collapse along the leading edge of the demonstrators.

"Sit!" yells Chris.

Everyone sits, breasts and penises jiggling. The line of officers takes a half-step forward, but their planned tactics have obviously been frustrated. The superior officer rushes forward but slides to a stop when he sees the cameras snap towards him. He shouts an order.

The police line moves forward and the officer at the center reaches for Chris' wrists. But Diane reaches her hands around Chris and begins to caress him below the waist. Suddenly there's something poking up between her fingers. The officer hesitates, trying to find an angle which will avoid touching Diane, and more importantly would avoid touching what she's caressing. He reaches forward again but Chris leans back against Diane, giving the officer a full view of Diane's hands moving up and down. The frustrated officer attempts a succession of angles to attack Chris's wrists, but none are viable. Other protesters join in with their own PDAs.

The other officers have continued to move forward and the outer ends of their line touches demonstrators all along the triangle. The other officers turn towards the officer fumbling with his arrest of Chris, casting sideways glances at other couples engaged in public displays of affection.

After several moment's hesitation, one of the officers on the right side of the triangle finally reaches down to attempt to pull Bassim's wrist towards him. Bassim's weight causes the officer to stumble and trip forward into the demonstrators and he is molested by several nude or scantily clad females, including Damini, before he can escape back outside the triangle. He is flushed and flustered. His uniform is in disheveled, especially below his belt buckle.

"Break!" yells a voice from the center of the triangle.

The couples at the base of the triangle spread out and around the ends of the police lines. Now the officers at the ends of the rope are surrounded—a roiling orgy in front of them and nude couples cooing and aahhing behind them, some reaching out and touching the policemen.

The officers retreat in disarray. None of the demonstrators have been attached to their zip ties. The superior police officer yells at his troop to do their duty. But by the time the rope has once again been pulled taut, the reporters have jumped in between the officers and the demonstrators and are interviewing everyone in sight.

When he spots a television crew marching towards him, the superior officer calls for a general retreat and the police officers scramble into their cars, maneuver around the press vans and speed off.

A cheer erupts from the demonstrators. They milled about, glorying in their nudity, glorying in their victory.

Chris turned to Diane. "Ready for a dip in the sea?" he asked, indicating a path leading away from the artificial reef.

She nodded and they quickly pulled on T-shirts, shorts and tights. In a moment, they were at the head of the path leading to the ocean. Diane turned around and looked back at Damini. The South East Asian's face formed a question. Diane angled her head towards the ocean. Damini tugged on her husband's arm. Diane angled her head towards the ocean again. When Diane was sure that the South East Asian couple was putting on their T-shirts to follow them, she skipped along the path to catch up to Chris.

At water's edge, Chris and Diane quickly stripped nude behind a tree and slipped into the warm water. They began slowly, gently using the fresh salt water to rub the sweat from their bodies. She was pleased to find his nipples hard beneath her fingers and his stomach harder. But she was especially gratified to find him already fully erect just at the thought of making love to her. Floating, she spread her legs wide and smiled as his hands moved up her right leg.

Diane's breasts flattened against her body, gravity's pull having been weakened by the ocean, making it difficult for Chris to grip enough to knead them. But the prominences of her nipples presented no such problem and he was able to squeeze hard while letting the lubrication of the salt water relieve any pain his twisting motions might cause her. He felt her lazily spread her legs and he slid his hand further up her right leg, intent on exploring all the pleasures usually concealed within her cracks.

Diane held on to him and spread her legs as far as they would go. She could relax in a moment, but only after his fingers had completed their thorough exploration. The first finger slipped up and back between her buttocks, locating her most private spot with ease. The fingertip tapped against the spot, turning her legs to jelly. Other fingers brushed against the bottom of her vulva, fluttering up and down her pussy lips. She felt her sex swell and start to warm the soft swirls of the ocean's waves.

Chris had found the promised land. From the way she clung to him, he knew that Diane was enjoying his fingers probing between her buttocks and along her pussy, he knew that she had abandoned all control to him. He pressed between the pucker at the center of her buttocks and felt her try to relax. But his probe of her back door was only a diversion and he slid two fingers inside her front door. She gasped and dug her fingers into his back.

His fingers brought mother ocean deep within her body, deep within her soul, deep within the passions gathering inside her sex. Her own heat, the heat of his fingers, the friction of his fingers plunging in, then pulling out, quickly brought her to a boil. She felt her clit burst forth from its covering as if to warm the entire sea.

She was floating now, barely holding onto him, joining the caresses of the sea. Chris used the hand behind her buttocks to hold her into place and slowly eased a finger inside her anus. Her muscles were too slack to resist him and his third finger slid easily inside the narrow canal. Outside and below her, his own arousal clamored for its own needs to be met, but he ignored it, content to exalt in his absolute dominion over her. He maneuvered her around to kiss him, completing his conquest by forcing her to hold onto his neck. She kissed him back hard, all inhibition having been vanquished.

And then as quickly as she'd allowed his fingers to invade her inner sanctuaries, she felt them withdraw, jerking her eyes open. No! wailed the cry within heart, but she dared not voice her complaint. She reached down for his rod, to urge it to fulfill her thoroughly aroused need. Her sex whimpered, protesting its disappointed desire. He held her back and she floated atop the softly undulating waves. She felt them tickle within her sex, but her needs cried out for a firmer touch than feathered ocean waves.

Her eyes looked up at him, pleading for more, but at that moment, all he wanted was to admire her beauty, her brown hair radiating out from her head, her blue eyes sparkling.

Her lips mouthed 'please' and he took mercy on her powerlessness. He lifted her up, her breasts bursting out of the water, her arms flailing for balance, her buttocks pressed against his midriff.

At that moment, they both saw the South East Asian couple on the beach intently watching them. Bassim appeared to be enjoying the spectacle. His wife appeared to be imagining herself in Chris's arms.

Chris reached up and caressed Diane's breasts as she slid onto him, as he impaled her sex atop his. "This is what you wanted, isn't it?"

"Yes," she moaned.

"To make love in the ocean."

"To be watched."

"Yes."

"To feel your entire body flush pink."

"Yes," she gasped.

"To yell your climax to the universe."

"No." But he was pumping her down below and she was aroused beyond any limit, any control and she was going to climax, no matter the circumstance. Hot pink had taken over her breasts and would soon seize the entire surface of her body.

"To yell your climax to the universe."

"No." But Diane knew he was right. Worse, *he* knew he was right.

She felt a clench down below and a deep rumble escape her throat. She heard his voice command her to, "Yell! Yell your climax to the universe!"

The clench whipped up her spine. "Yes!" she shouted. "Yes! Yes! Yes!" Yes with each wave, yes with each uncontrollable pulse, yes with each spasm of pleasure. "*Yes!*" with the eyes of the couple on the beach transfixed upon her. And most of all, "Yes!" with Chris' hot come spurting inside her.

As she subsided, the South East Asian couple slowly shuffled off.

"Why was that so hot for you?" asked Chris.

"Taboo, breaking all the rules."

"Not reuniting with mother ocean?"

"That too. Even more, reuniting with you."

That night, back at Hedo, Chris and Diane ate late and watched the show, a mixture of singing, acrobatics and suggestive shenanigans. The night's theme was rock-star. Several men were in KISS regalia, complete with white-face make-up. Several women were dressed as Madonna. Diane relaxed her head into Chris' chest as they sipped cognac.

"What happened after we went our separate ways?" Her voice was wistful.

He assumed she was asking for information. "I worked for a few firms, started my own company, lost most of it in the divorce, now I'm foreman at an international firm. I've been to the Gulf, Canada, Europe, Asia." He felt her body tense. It was subtle, but she was now engaged.

"What did you do in Mexico?"

"Not that gulf. Abu Dhabi. What about you?"

"Same. Marriage. Divorce. Worked my way up the partner track at the law firm. Interesting cases, my choice."

"Ever wonder what would have happened if things had been different?"

"All the time." He felt her relax against him.

What would life have been with Diane, he wondered. They had gone their separate ways because he would be travelling. He would be working with his hands, she her brain. The hours would be long, for both of them. They were afraid it wouldn't work out. She had married another lawyer, he a pretty accounts clerk at a construction supply firm. They had played it safe. Their marriages had slowly disintegrated. Maybe they would have tried harder if they'd married each other.

Chris shut his eyes and imagined Diane pregnant with their second child as he nailed the last wallboard in place on their new house, imagined them falling asleep together as they always had, as they always would. He jerked his eyes open. Diane was asleep, in the here and now. Maybe coming together this week was a second chance, a new opportunity, was the universe weaving their life paths back together...

Chapter 3

At lunch, Bassim suggested that they have fresh-cooked pasta. Damini suspected that this was to facilitate a serious discussion on some topic and she feared that Bassim was finally going to confront her about her recent—and her first in twelve years of marriage—indiscretion. With a plate piled full of steaming pasta, there would be no need to interrupt their conversation to return to the buffet.

But all Bassim had wanted to talk about over lunch was the perennial problem of persistent puddles in their back yard. Damini wished he hadn't piled their plates so high; they could both afford to lose weight, him especially. But at least he hadn't wanted to discuss Eric.

After lunch, Bassim smacked his lips. "How about we find a quiet spot to read?" he asked.

She readily agreed, though she suspected that after a few paragraphs she'd end up shutting her book and lazing in the sun. However, when they paused for drinks at the bar, Damini noticed that her husband was not carrying anything to read. Fears knotted her stomach. When the bartender raised the bottle of rum to top off her Mojito, she waved him off. She would need all her wits about her.

Bassim led them to a quiet nook by a small pool under the walkway. There were two beach chairs. Anyone walking above would be unable to hear them.

Damini lifted her oversized T-shirt off over her head. Her bright blue bikini contrasted perfectly with her dark brown skin. When she was selling real estate, she braided her straight black hair, but today it flowed freely halfway down her back. Although she was in her early forties, she was curvaceous and fit. While ordinarily she would be enjoying putting her body on display for all to see, at the present moment she felt only a need to be totally vulnerable for what was to come, a need to have the impending conversation done. Done for once and for all.

Bassim was wearing a pair of shorts that doubled as bathing trunks, but he hadn't envisioned this discussion taking place in swimwear. Nevertheless, he felt obliged to match his wife's action and he too removed his T-shirt. He was big in every way, standing six feet tall with ripples of flab on his belly. And the flab on his arms and legs made them look bigger than would have his muscles alone. He had a full head of hair with only a few flecks of grey and he felt this was perfect for his forty-eight years. At the school where he was principal, everyone found him handsome and charismatic, especially when there was a sparkle in his deep brown eyes. His wife looked especially alluring in her skimpy blue bikini but sorrow kept him from being aroused by her beauty.

He stood, ignoring the plastic beach chairs which beckoned below. If she sat, he would postpone the conversation to another day. But she did not sit, rather she looked up at him. She didn't have to look too far up as she was only three inches shorter than her husband, but she did have to angle her head backwards.

"This thing between you and Eric Agnarson," Bassim began, "is deeply hurtful."

"I'm sorry," she said.

"Sorry is for me and I accept it. And I forgive you." He sat down and she followed him to the beach chairs. He leaned back and extended his legs along the length of the chair and she copied his posture.

Bassim paused, gathering his thoughts. Damini wished that he would just let loose, yell, scream—even beat her—instead of torturing her with his calm and benevolent acceptance.

"But shame is for yourself. Are you ashamed at what you have done?"

"I am ashamed that I have hurt you. I am ashamed that I went behind your back."

"As well you should be," he said, a note of ominous finality in his voice. Bassim sat up and put his feet on the ground, another clear indication that this was the end of the conversation. He started to stand.

"But."

Her voice froze him just short of standing fully upright.

"But I am not ashamed for being a woman," she continued, "for having desires, for having..."

"I have always—"

"Yes you have."

He slumped back onto the chair.

Damini took a deep breath. "It started innocently enough—he was at an open house. They didn't have an agent so I wanted to sign them up. When the wife was in the washroom, I suggested to him that we meet for dinner to discuss their needs. I figured they would attend as a couple.

"But Eric came alone. He's skinny, likes to run. And he's short." This was not the truth, Eric was tall and had worn a sports jacket that had fit his lean but muscular body perfectly. But her husband didn't need to know these details. Eric's golden hair had covered his ears, but not his mischievous smile or sky-blue eyes. When he'd pulled out the chair for her to sit, it was as if he was about to wrap his body around hers.

She swallowed, then continued, intent on putting all the details out in the open. "It started out innocently—sharing secrets, sexting, once phone sex."

"Innocently—how was this *innocent*?"

"We were just talking."

"And when you were 'just talking' what did you say to each other?"

"I told him about the time we locked ourselves out of the house and had to sleep in the garage."

He remembered that night, sleeping on an air mattress, cuddling together to escape the cold, making love. She still referred to it as the time '*we* locked ourselves out' despite the fact that it had been entirely his fault. He'd locked the door to the house even though they were both just outside in the garden, and had then dropped his keys through the sewer grate. That was the night she'd forgiven him all his faults, the night they'd told each other their deepest secrets, the night they'd wordlessly pledged undying and unconditional allegiance to each other. They had had oral sex in the 69 position and exhausted everything they could recall from the *Kama Sutra*.

"Did you tell him—"

"Just that we had to sleep outside."

"Not what we…"

"No." She had told Eric *everything* about that night, but telling Bassim would only heap hurt upon hurt.

He was silent for a moment. To her, waiting for a response, it seemed an eternity.

"That was our secret." There was sadness in his voice, but no rebuke. Why, a voice cried inside her, why can't he be *angry*?

"The phone sex, what was that like?" he asked.

29

"It was one afternoon," she began, remembering that it had in fact been many afternoons and even one night when Bassim was hosting a parent/teachers' event. "I took off some of my clothes." She decided to leave out the fact that she had in fact removed *all* her clothes. "He said he was touching himself and he told me to touch myself."

"Did you?"

She nodded.

"Where?"

"You know." She remembered how wonderful her fingers had felt on her breasts and nipples, on her pubic mound, between her lips, inside, and on her clit. How she'd been so *hot*, so wet, so *aroused*.

"Did you climax?" His voice was flat, as if he was asking her about the dry cleaning.

"Bassim!"

"Did you?" At last she heard a hint of hardness in his voice. She felt relief and dread all at the same time.

"Yes, I came." But when she saw the hurt on his face, she quickly added, "But it wasn't as good as when you touch me." That much was true—her own touch was effective enough, but not as exciting as someone else touching her and not *nearly* as exciting as when Eric had told her to imagine that it was his finger between her pussy lips, his finger stroking up and down, his finger *inside* her.

"And after innocently?" She heard his voice crack.

"We went to a hotel."

"What happened at in the hotel?

"Bassim!"

"What *happened*?" He slammed his hand on the arm of the chair and she heard the sound of plastic snapping. But the chair did not collapse.

"We had *sex*!" Their eyes locked, pain searing them together. She did her best to expel the memories from her mind, how attentive to her needs Eric had been, how he'd used his athletic body, how his eyes sparkled when he'd seen the reactions he was provoking. No! today was for Bassim, *not* Eric!

"What kind of *sex*?" He infected the word with anger, derision and accusation.

She lowered her eyes. "All kinds."

The silence hung heavy, as if Bassim was trying to crush her with it. Her breath became shallower and shallower until he interrupted it. "Does Eric's wife know?"

"No."

"And I suppose that he's young, and handsome and powerful?"

She shook her head. Eric was all of these things, but it would only hurt Bassim to admit it.

"And your *needs*, you are saying it will happen again? This shameful, this *hurtful* behavior?"

She shook her head. She wondered whether she was wrong to shake her head. She and Eric had agreed to meet again when she returned back north. "But please, can't we have more excitement in our lives?"

Bassim looked at his wife, saw the hurt in her eyes. A husband should please his wife. Perhaps this had been his fault. Perhaps they did need more excitement. "Yes," he said, nodding. "What kind of excitement?" He held his breath, afraid of her answer.

"We don't have to swing with other couples." She saw the relief in her husband's eyes and knew it had been the right thing to say. If only he had been willing to swing. Maybe then their relationship would open up to new things. Truly *exciting* things. "They have a room where there are people having sex."

"Damini! Surely not an orgy, surely…"

She heard his voice crack. A grown man, his voice cracking. But she wasn't about to give up. "Some people are just watching. We don't have to do anything. Please. Let's just go, see what it's like."

He nodded, not at all liking what he had just agreed to. The nude beach was bad enough. He had barely withstood watching the couple in the ocean at a distance. But people in the same room actually…

That night Damini managed to lead her husband to the Romping Room. By day, it was part of the spa. But, after darkness settled, it transformed into a free-sex zone. She led him first into a small room with an X-shaped cross on which she stood, hoping that her husband would tie her to it, but he failed to get the hint. At the far end, atop a large purple velvet couch, a couple was making out. Damini could tell that her husband was uncomfortable being so close to another couple who, in his words, "were doing it".

Bassim had worn a black shirt and black dress pants, having refused to wear the bright yellow shirt she'd bought him. Damini had done her best to make their attire conform to the resort's Jamaican Colours theme-night with a yellow shirt and green skirt.

She led her husband back out into the main area, a large courtyard. Along the side of one wall were several mattresses on the floor. Against the wall to the right were three chaises. To the left were two small pools and one larger one. Above and slightly offset from the pools were two alcoves which allowed good sight lines but also a modicum of privacy.

Damini and Bassim gravitated to the far alcove and she set him down on the large leatherette chaise inside. She kissed him, but his kiss back was perfunctory. She positioned herself beside her husband and they watched a young Japanese couple making out in the far corner of the main area. His shorts and her skirt were black; his shirt was green, hers gold. They were kissing passionately. One of his hands was on her breast, the other between her legs. One of her hands was holding his head close to hers, the other was caressing the top of his shorts.

Damini began to massage along the zipper of Bassim's pants. She was pleased to feel him beginning to swell. The young Japanese couple had removed their shirts.

Damini watched her husband continuing to watch the young couple. She wanted to join in his watching, to comment on the woman stroking the man's hard-on, but she knew that if she spoke, she might disturb her husband's concentration. Instead, she slowly unzipped his pants and pulled them down a few inches. Bassim was fully erect and she pulled his loose boxer shorts up and over his penis. She carefully slid her panties to the floor, making sure that her husband did not see what she was doing.

The young Japanese couple continued to make out and Bassim stirred as he caught glimpses of forbidden flesh. They were making rhythmic stroking motions.

Damini's plan was to climb atop her husband and to take his penis into her vagina. They would be making love *in public*! Her head would be to one side and he could continue to watch the young Japanese couple. They had removed their shirts and he was sucking on her nipples. But when she straddled Bassim, his concentration was broken and his erection softened.

"They're so young," he complained.

"Relax, enjoy," she pleaded.

The young Japanese woman had lifted her mate's shorts and was kissing the top of his erection. Damini saw that Bassim was once again watching them and she slid her own mouth over Bassim's penis. He was immediately hard again.

Damini straddled her husband, positioning the tip of his penis between her tingling pussy lips. A jolt of electricity shot up her spine. He was in an inch. It was *happening!* She slid further.

But two new couples entered the space, laughing uproariously at a joke told outside. Damini felt Bassim go soft and flop outside her. She turned to watch the newcomers. One couple was thin and white, the other muscular and black. The white couple kissed, the black couple kissed. Then they exchanged partners. Green, gold and black clothing was quickly removed. Mouths joined. Hands caressed. Damini wished she and Bassim could be part of that burgeoning sexuality. She stroked her husband's shaft, trying to urge it back into the action.

The black man brought the white woman into the pool in front of them where she took his erection into his mouth. Then he turned her around so that her head faced the side of the pool, and plunged himself inside her.

Damini tried every trick she knew. But Bassim's penis failed to respond to her touch, failed to respond to her lips, failed to respond to her mouth, failed to respond to both of her hands together.

"Let's go back to our room," Bassim suggested.

Damini wanted to plead to stay, but the soft flesh in her hands told her that there was no point. As they left, she took one last look at the orgy roiling behind her. So close, but so, so far.

Back in their room, Bassim recovered his manhood and he was able to climb atop her. As he thrust back and forth, Damini's mind floated back to the Romping Room, imagining herself with the white man, then with the black man, then with both. She felt her husband begin to come and she imagined being back in the Romping Room, inserting the tip of his penis into her vagina. But this time he remained hard and she slid all the way down his shaft. The thought made her hot and she began to join in her husband's lovemaking. But then he shuddered and stopped. She pressed upwards urging him on, but he managed only two more thrusts before falling beside her and descending quickly into sleep.

Damini stared up at the mirror in the ceiling, at her corpulent husband snoring beside her, at her breasts slowly rising and falling. Bassim had tried. But her lungs ached with need. A tear rolled down her cheek. She looked deeper into the mirror.

Chapter 4

Amanda was just coming out of the shower when there was a knock at the door. She opened the door and saw a porter and a black woman standing on the walkway. Amanda estimated that the woman was several inches shorter than herself.

The petite black woman stepped forward and extended her hand, "Hi, I'm Helen."

Amanda shook her hand while eying the two large suitcases the porter was wheeling through the door. "But this is my room."

Helen looked around the room. There were two queen-sized beds. Only the one closest to the door had been slept in. Then she returned her gaze to Amanda. "My travel agent said that she'd arranged a reduced rate. Double occupancy. With another woman."

Amanda's eyes went wide, then she nodded. "It's just that this is the second day I've been here and…" Her towel slipped, letting one of her large round breasts pop out. The rest of her body was tanned, but not the errant breast. She quickly readjusted her towel over her breasts, then motioned to the porter. "Please put the bags by the far bed." She extended her hand toward Helen, then realized that would put her in danger of losing her towel again. She held her arm close to her body and gave a half wave. "Amanda."

As soon as the porter had left, Amanda scooped out the clothes she'd deposited in the left side of the dresser and quickly stuffed them in the bottom drawer of the right side. "I haven't had a roomie since college," she apologized.

Helen smiled, "That couldn't have been that long ago."

Amanda vaguely registered Helen's remark as a compliment as she propped herself up on her bed and watched Helen unpack. First was a white leather bustier and matching thong. On Amanda, it would blend in with her skin but against Helen's ebony skin, the contrast would be exotic. Next out of the suitcase was sheer white bra and panty set. Then similar in red. Amanda resolved not to let the attractive black woman see her own very, very ordinary underwear.

The rest of Helen's lingerie was so small and skimpy as to be almost invisible and Amanda concentrated on the smaller black woman herself. She estimated Helen to be in her early thirties and no more than five foot three inches high. She was skinny, her breasts only slight mounds atop her chest and her hips were barely wider than her waist. Her short black hair was curly, tight atop her head. She held her body like a coiled spring.

"What brings you to Hedonism?" asked Amanda.

"I'm studying the resort. Resorts and hotels in Jamaica, but Hedonism II in particular. You?"

"Mostly just to have fun."

"And the rest?"

"I need to work out a few issues."

Helen pulled out a purple vibrator and waved it back and forth. "Everyone has issues." She looked up and down the blonde woman's full figure. "You have a wonderful body. Do you work out?"

Amanda nodded. "I'm a personal trainer."

Helen pulled a dress out of her suitcase. It was made of stretchy material with bands of yellow, black and green color around it. Amanda imagined how delectable Helen would look with Jamaica's national colors clinging to her every curve. "I bet you look spectacular in that," Amanda told her.

"It'd look even better on you." Helen tossed the dress towards Amanda and it landed just in front of her on the bed. "Go ahead, try it on."

"It's too small for me."

"It's one size fits all. Go ahead. *You'll* look *spectacular*."

"But I'll stretch it."

Amanda watched Helen's brown eyes look her up and down, her strikingly angular features and full lips forming an admiring smile.

Helen shrugged. "It's a risk worth taking."

Amanda hesitated. Wearing someone else's clothes? Besides she was nude under her towel and she'd just met Helen. But her roommate's bright-eyed smile overcame her concerns.

Amanda rose from the bed and carefully shed her towel as she held her body sideways to avoid putting too much of herself on display.

The petite black woman chuckled inwardly at her bunk-buddy's affectation of modesty. And Amanda might have been even more uptight if she knew how much the sight of her voluptuous curves and ponderous breasts was turning Helen on. Helen clenched her sex tight; she'd have to take it slow if she was going to be able to explore Amanda up close. As Amanda pulled the dress over her head, Helen peeked around her side. In between Amanda's wide hips was a thin strip of blonde curls with a heart tattoo just to the left—where it would have been covered by hair if Amanda had let her bush grow wild.

Amanda pulled the dress down her body and turned towards Helen. Her long blonde hair cascaded over her shoulders and onto the dress, contrasting beautifully with the black and green stripes. Her blue eyes sparkled as she inspected herself in the mirror. She turned to Helen, "What do you think?"

"You look magnificent!" And she did. The dress clung to her curves, the bands of color emphasizing the bulge of her breasts, the inward curve of her waist, the outward arc of her hips, the inward incline of her legs.

Helen touched Amanda's arm and felt a surge of electricity. Had the white goddess felt it? Helen withdrew her hand and watched Amanda holding her body with the confidence of an athlete as she slowly pirouetted. Her ass was even more luscious than the rest of her. Helen wanted to jump her, to push her to the bed, to—but she'd have to restrain herself if she wanted to land Amanda.

As Amanda completed her turn, the two women locked eyes. Helen slowly stripped out of her travel clothes. Amanda averted her gaze when the black woman started to remove her bra.

"What should I wear to the beach?" asked Helen, forcing Amanda to look up to watch her as she searched through her dresser drawers.

Amanda choked back a gasp. The petite black woman was even more beautiful unclothed. "The nude beach is closest," she stuttered.

Helen stood and grinned. "One less decision."

The black woman's brashness made Amanda regret her comment about the nude beach being closer.

Helen smiled at Amanda's discomfiture as the taller woman realized that she'd have to remove the dress. Her smile widened as the dress was slowly lifted past the curve of her hips, revealing the tattoo once more. Helen's smile widened all the way across her face as Amanda's breasts bounced free.

At the nude beach, Amanda and Helen found a pair of lounge chairs a bit back from the water's edge and watched people stroll along the beach. Boobs bounced and willies wiggled. Chris and Diane ambled by wearing their 'Save the Reef' T-shirts, but nothing else. "What's up with that?" asked Helen.

"It's a protest against a new development which they say threatens the reef reclamation project."

Keiko and Yoshi tottered in the other direction, carrying food back to their chairs. Their bodies were completely shaven; not a wisp of hair anywhere. "They've never had sex with anyone else," remarked Helen.

"How do you know?" Keiko's penis was slightly engorged and swinging back and forth.

"Look at how easy they are with each other, how tentative they are in looking at other nude bodies, embarrassed, intrigued, and making sure the other doesn't see them looking. And look closely between their legs. It's the first time they've shaved."

Amanda looked closely at Keiko's crotch. There were several little pink nicks. Maybe Helen was right. She turned away and pointed towards a white couple in their forties, both lean, he with dark brown hair, hers dyed blonde, flirting with another couple. "Not them. By the end of the week, those two will have laid everything on two feet."

"Swingers?" asked Helen.

Amanda nodded. "She even tried to pick me up."

"And?"

The two women looked at each other, not sure where to take that line of conversation.

Damini and Bassim strolled by. Helen pointed to the South East Asian woman: "She's hot to trot."

"How can you tell?"

"The sway of her hips."

Amanda wondered about the sway of her own hips.

Helen pointed to a couple who were making out atop the floating offshore platform. "Now that's a PDA!" The couple was kissing, her hand grazing up and down his very erect erection.

"What's a 'PDA'?"

"Public display of affection."

Two men, holding hands walked by.

"I didn't know that gays were allowed in Jamaica," queried

Amanda.

"Hedonism welcomes everyone," noted Helen. "They've even hosted Bloom, a gay festival. Elsewhere on the island, there's still a lot of homophobia, but the government is making strides. However, you're right, other resorts probably wouldn't allow gays, at least not openly."

"How do you know all this?"

"It's my job to know. My employer is considering investing in Jamaica. Head office wants to know what works, what doesn't."

"Is that why you came to Hedo?"

"That's part of the reason." She grazed her finger down Amanda's arm.

Amanda shivered, but did not pull away. Instead she pointed to two women coming from the other direction and joining the gay couple. "What about lesbians?"

"They're less of a concern. Jamaica's macho culture would just like to pretend they don't exist. Besides, lesbians are more compatible with the swingers who love to come to Hedo."

"Why swingers?"

"Male swingers are fine with their wives being bi-sexual, but they're very uptight about their own sexuality."

"Oh."

"What about you?" asked Helen.

"Me?"

"What's your attitude towards lesbians?"

Amanda sighed. "I'm still working that out."

"Do you like being with men?"

"Yes." Amanda's face flushed pink.

"Have you ever been with a woman?"

"Once. A long time ago..."

When it was clear that Amanda intended to keep the rest of that story to herself, Helen rose to her feet. "Let's go for a swim," she proposed, pulling her roommate up.

In the water, Amanda was the slower swimmer and Helen dove around her like a dolphin. Once she did a swan dive right in front of Amanda giving her a full view of not only the curves but also of all the inner parts of her bottom. Water rushing along the slit of pink in the middle of chocolate thighs provoked a tingle in the blonde's own sex.

Back in their room, Helen released her towel to the floor and pointed to the bathroom. "We need to wash the salt water off our bodies."

"It's okay. You go first."

"I hear the showers are big enough for two."

"But—"

Helen pulled Amanda's towel off her body causing her large breasts to jiggle slightly. "And that they have multi-directional jets."

Amanda swallowed and allowed Helen to push her into the washroom. In the mirror, Amanda caught a sight of the small black woman's teeth glistening within her smile. She was truly beautiful.

Inside the shower stall, Helen shut the door behind them and turned on the showerhead. Amanda felt the water warm on her skin as it washed the salt away. Then she moved aside to let the water splash off Helen's skin.

Helen handed her the shampoo and Amanda poured a dollop into her cupped hand, then moved it towards the top of her blonde tresses. But Helen's hand on her arm stopped her. "Do me," she said, pointing to the short black curls atop her own head.

Amanda gingerly dribbled shampoo onto Helen's head. The black woman's curls were tight and it took effort to massage the shampoo in. But at last she was satisfied and pulled Helen under the shower to wash the shampoo out of her hair. Their bodies brushed against each other and Amanda felt a jolt of excitement. She wondered whether Helen felt the same way. She wondered whether it was normal to be excited by a woman in the same way she was excited by a man.

Helen motioned to Amanda to bend down. As she did, she felt a small drop of cold and then Helen's hands spreading the shampoo into her hair, Helen's hands gathering the long strands of her hair atop her head, Helen's hands kneading the shampoo into her hair, Helen's finger's massaging her scalp, Helen's fingertips sending tingles down her spine. The scent of jasmine from the shampoo filled the shower.

Amanda washed the shampoo from her hair and opened her eyes. Helen was holding a bar of soap out for her to take. Amanda hesitated. Clearly the ebony angel meant for her own body to be washed. Shampoo on the head was one thing. But... Helen slowly, with infinite gentleness, pressed the soap into Amanda's hand. Then she drew

Amanda's hand forward pressing the soap on her shoulder, well above her breast. Helen's body was hotter than the jets of the shower beating on Amanda's back.

Helen let her hand drop away leaving Amanda's hand all alone pressing the ivory white soap against her dark skin. Amanda began to softly rub the soap along Helen's shoulder. She saw the other woman's nipples pucker. Had she done that?!? Amanda soaped lower, being careful to go up and over Helen's breasts, but her fingers brushed against the hard black nipple. Helen moaned. Amanda felt her own nipples pucker.

Helen turned to face the wall and Amanda vigorously lathered her back, paying special care to clean Helen's ripe round buttocks. Helen jutted her butt out. Amanda tentatively brought the soap to the top of her butt cheeks and pressed it between them. Helen spread her legs. Amanda pushed the soap in further and gave Helen a thorough cleaning inside.

The black woman quickly turned around and Amanda was pressing the soap on the hard round curls of her pubic hair. Helen pushed her hand down and Amanda felt the soap press between Helen's pussy lips.

"That feels good, baby," Helen encouraged. Then she took the soap from Amanda's hand and began to lather the blonde's large bosom. *She* made no effort to avoid the pink nipples. Amanda gasped. "We're just getting started, baby," Helen purred, using her free hand to spread the soap on the undersides of Amanda's mammaries.

Amanda felt herself being turned around, the bar of soap sliding all over her bum. Against her better judgment, she spread her legs and immediately the bar of soap was between her buttocks. Where Amanda had used only the bar of soap to do the cleaning, Helen probed with her fingers. No one had ever touched her there before. Never, never in her deep dark place! But Helen's tiny probing fingers were at once deviant and delicious. She felt a deep moan rumble up from her lungs and out her throat.

Helen's hand on her hip told Amanda it was time to turn around. Helen teased the soap just above Amanda's pubic bone, drawing it back and forth, down centimeter by centimeter, until it was lathering the blonde's remaining wisps of pubic hair. Then it slid, slowly, but inexorably, down the center of Amanda's body, brushing against her clit.

"Jesus!" gasped Amanda.

"Do you want me to stop?" But Helen hadn't paused for an answer and the soap was sliding between Helen's pussy lips.

Amanda bit her lip and shut her eyes to stop her knees from buckling as Helen drew the soap lightly back and forth all along her sex. Then the soap was no longer there and Amanda heard it hit the floor below. She steeled herself for the sensation of small black fingers stimulating her most sensitive parts.

But there was nothing. She opened her eyes to see Helen fiddling with the shower controls. Suddenly water jetted out from all angles. Helen twirled her body to quickly remove all the soap from her glistening skin, all the while keeping her eyes fixed, her hungry, hungry eyes, fixed on Amanda.

Amanda's own attention was transfixed on the water droplets bouncing off the dark skin of the lithe beauty with whom she was sharing the shower. Even though they were no longer standing next to each other, she could feel Helen's heat against her own skin.

Then the last speck of soap on Helen's skin was gurgling down the drain and the smaller woman adjusted the direction of the jets to rinse Amanda's flushed skin—pink from being washed, pink from the hot water jets beating against it, pink from unabashed sexual arousal. Helen made sure that one jet was angled between Amanda's butt crack and another was directed at the center her sex.

The sensations were amazing, pushing Amanda's arousal almost to the point of no return. She did her best to steady herself against the wall of the shower. And that was all the opening Helen needed. The black woman pressed herself tightly against her larger companion. One nipple was hard between her lips, the other hot against her fingers. She licked the tip of the nipple inside her mouth and felt her lips smile at the moan escaping from above.

Helen let the fingers of her free hand dance down Amanda's torso. The involuntary tightening of the larger woman's belly muscles told her that she had overcome her resistance, a fact which was confirmed by the hardness of her love button, the arousal of her pussy lips and the welcome slipperiness between.

Heat radiated down Amanda's body even before Helen's fingers arrived. Puckering suction on her nipple stoked the flames and flushed her skin. Delicate little fingers probing Amanda's clit drew the heat downwards. Surely she— But the fingers slid lower and Amanda felt her pussy lips cry out for release as Helen's fingers teased them. If only the fingers would press harder, maybe she could come. But surely Helen wouldn't—

Helen pressed her fingers between Amanda's pale pink pussy lips and gloated her victory when she was greeted with feminine slipperiness.

"Don't," pleaded Amanda.

Helen continued to stroke in and out. "Don't what?" she challenged.

"Don't," moaned Amanda.

"You want me stop?" Helen stroked Amanda's wetness up her engorged pussy lips, around her clit, and back inside her pussy. Amanda shuddered and Helen felt a twinge between her own legs.

"Don't," whispered Amanda.

Helen inserted two fingers inside and felt the spongy ridges of Amanda's inner love-button. "Don't what?" she teased.

"Please," exhaled Amanda.

Helen curled her fingers, stroking all along the ridged areas. Amanda gasped and Helen sensed her fingers being squeezed. "Do you want me to stop?" she whispered.

But Amanda was too far gone to breathe, let alone to verbalize a response. Helen stroked harder and faster. Amanda's fingernails dug into her back and her pussy mashed her knuckles together.

"Shit!" screamed Amanda.

Helen felt contraction after contraction grip her fingers. When she could, she thrust her fingers as deep as they would go inside Amanda's pussy and then, when the next contraction receded, she pulled her fingers out as far as she could without losing the sensation of her lover's arousal.

The first contraction had almost broken Amanda in two. The rest had whipped up her spine every time Helen had crooked her fingers. When Helen had changed to a thrusting motion, Amanda had begun to recover enough control to breathe, to fully savor the warm waves of pleasure cascading up and down her body. There was a new smell inside the shower: salty and pungent.

Amanda opened her eyes and smiled at Helen. "I told you to stop," she complained.

"But you didn't want me to stop, did you?"

"You have to be punished," said Amanda, ignoring the objection.

"Punished?"

"You took my breath away. Now I'm going to take yours."

"Just try," laughed Helen, scooting out of the shower.

But Amanda caught up to her and threw the smaller woman onto the bed. They wrestled briefly, breasts jiggling, legs askew, but Amanda quickly got the upper hand, turned her butt towards Helen's face and mashed her sex down against her lips. Amanda knew that Helen couldn't breathe and that she'd soon have to release her—

But Helen wasn't breathing, she wasn't even *trying* to breathe. Helen was *licking*! Right up Amanda's slit. And Helen was sucking her clit in and out of her mouth. She licked back down and poked her tongue inside. Amanda held onto the hips writhing beneath her. In spite of herself, Amanda shivered with delight.

Amanda felt Helen's tongue flick her clit, could feel her arousal deepen and pulled herself up to escape the clutches of Helen's sexual dominion. "You have to be punished!" she gasped.

"The only punishment is to do to me what I did to you, to your *insides*." Helen own insides called out, their yearning deep, demanding, insistent.

Amanda felt Helen's fingers probing her sex. She pushed her arm away, then decided that pushing her own fingers inside Helen would be the *perfect* revenge. She probed between the darker than dark pussy lips until she found pink. Even though she'd only pressed lightly, her finger easily slipped inside.

Helen felt her yearning deepen, spread throughout her body. But the heat from Amanda's finger was only probing, not stimulating. Two could play at explorer, and the Amazonian goddess above her was still *ripe* for exploration!

Behind her, Amanda felt a finger slide into her own pussy and she had to stop herself from falling down against the smaller woman beneath her. Then there was another finger—two fingers—inside her pussy and she inserted two of her own into Helen. Amanda nuzzled Helen's pussy and almost choked on the pungent odors. But in a moment she began to enjoy the smell and dipped her tongue in for a taste. It was oysters and caviar, but stronger than any she'd ever tasted.

Amanda felt Helen try to lift her head towards her own pussy, but she positioned her calves on Helen's shoulders to prevent the effort. Amanda purred as she licked and fondled Helen's sex. Amanda smiled as she held her own pussy close to Helen's lips, but just out of reach. Such would be Helen's punishment.

Then Amanda felt fingers slip along the crack between her buttocks. One found her ass and gently pressed. What the—?!? The finger left, but was back, warm and wet. And it was slipping inside. All the way up her ass!

Two could play that game! Amanda slid a third finger from her left hand into Helen's pussy and the longest finger of her right hand all the way inside Helen's back door, one-upping the three smaller fingers Helen had inside her. Helen moaned and Amanda stroked harder doing her best to stifle her own moan.

Amanda had to pee. But she wasn't going to stop now. Not when she had Helen moaning beneath her. Not when she had Helen's hips pushing rhythmically against her fingers. Amanda stroked with the fingers she had in the black woman's pussy. She licked around her clit and up and down her pussy lips. She pulled the finger she inside Helen's ass in and out. The aroma from Helen's sex intoxicated Amanda's nostrils.

Amanda's urge to pee was getting stronger. But she was also sexually aroused. She'd never had to pee when she'd been horny before. But Helen was sucking little gasps of breath beneath her. The little black pussy was tightening, her ass was loosening. And Helen was *hot*! Amanda felt a little shudder against her fingers.

Less than a minute and she'd have the little bitch. *Then* she could pee. She'd stop just as Helen was beginning her orgasm. Exerting her power, then withdrawing it—the perfect revenge! But Amanda could feel her own orgasm building as well. After she'd peed, she'd sit back down on Helen's face—take another climax without giving one to Helen!

Helen shuddered, hotter than hot, clenching Amanda's fingers— all three of her fingers. Amanda had never been so turned on in her life

45

feeling the little black woman beneath her, completely in her power, shuddering contraction after contraction—contractions she herself had caused!

Amanda readied to withdraw but suddenly her eyes were wrenched open and her neck snapped back. Her sex was twisted so tight it felt as if it would shatter into little pieces. But instead of shattering, it exploded in hot waves of heat, wave after wave of pleasure so powerful that the crest of each wave hurt, actually hurt. But such a *delicious* hurt! And she was spurting—she was peeing! Peeing! Searing hot pee every time her orgasm crested. How *disgusting*! Even if it *was* on top of Helen.

Amanda jumped off, dashed into the bathroom and came back with a towel. Helen was making little patterns with the liquid atop her belly. Some had dribbled onto the sheets.

Amanda cleaned Helen off. "Sorry."

"Sorry for what?"

"For peeing on you. Uk!" Was Helen really this *dense*?

"That wasn't pee."

"What?"

"That was your come."

"Women don't have come."

"Not all women, but *you* do."

"Women don't—"

Helen took her fingers and rubbed them on the sheets where Amanda's ejaculate had leaked. She smelled her fingers, then held them towards Amanda's nose. "That wasn't pee."

Amanda took a whiff. It didn't smell like urine. It didn't even *look* like urine.

Chapter 5

"Have you seen anyone worthwhile?" asked Charles as he watched Carmen survey the main dining area. Charles and Carmen were veteran swingers on the prowl. There were several other swingers at the resort with whom they could hook up, but that night he and his wife were looking for new playmates. Charles—only Carmen and his other lovers called him Charlie—knew that his wife would have the final say so he wanted to draw out her opinion first.

Charles and Carmen Johnson were a white couple in their forties. They were both lean and ran to keep in shape. Charles had some muscle on him from weight training, but not so much as to slow him down. Carmen had recently had breast augmentation surgery and held herself straight to show off her new acquisitions. He was handsome—perfect bait—with dark brown hair and even darker brown eyes to match. Atop Carmen's head, her hair was dyed blonde; she removed every last follicle elsewhere with a personal laser device. Her eyes were grey. Atop her pubic bone was a tattoo of a snake slithering downwards. As always, she had carefully applied a coat of deep red lipstick to her almost constantly smiling lips. Twenty years ago she had been pretty; now she had emerged into an attractive beauty.

The experienced swingers were at the corner of the resort's main dining area. It was a large room which looped around and in front of the stage to the couple's right. In front of the stage and below the main level was a dance floor. The buffet and bar were at the far end of the room. Dinner was mostly over, but the dining area was half full of guests waiting for the evening stage show.

"Ready for some action?" asked Carmen.

He nodded.

It was Toga Night at the resort and they, like about a third of the guests, were dressed in the ancient Roman costume. Half of the toga-wearers had costumes composed of their bed sheets. The other half, which included Carmen and Charlie, had brought their own custom-tailored versions. As usual, Carmen's attire covered the bare minimum of her flesh.

"What about that cute Asian couple?" she asked, pointing to Yoshi and Keiko who were sitting alone at a large table.

"Japanese," he specified. Her intended targets were dressed only in bed sheets and their lack of creativity gave him pause. "They're okay. Do you think they'd be interested?"

She nodded. "The first day at the beach, she kept her bottom on. But at the demonstration, they went fully nude and even engaged in a naughty PDA."

Carmen and Charlie quickly inspected themselves to make sure nothing was out of place. She adjusted her white string bikini to better support her now very large breasts. She turned so that Charlie could tighten it and tie it securely behind her back. Below she had a thin band of soft cotton, a cross between a toga and a miniskirt with a thong underneath. Everything was white. In contrast, Charles was wearing a flowing robe of purple velveteen—the discredited colors of the tyrant kings. All he had beneath was a matching purple thong.

Carmen led the way—it was less threatening to be approached by a female—and when she arrived beside Yoshi and Keiko, she pointed at two of the vacant seats. "Is it okay if we join you?" she asked Yoshi. It was open seating so she didn't really need to ask, but swinger strategy was based on getting as many positive answers as possible.

The young Japanese woman nodded.

At that moment, the show started on stage. The first act was a band playing a rousing reggae number. As soon as the music stopped, Carmen introduced herself and the two couples exchanged names.

The next act featured two scantily-clad black performers pouring milk over each other. Carmen pointed to the bulge in the male performer's thong, "Yoshi, wouldn't you like to spend the night with him?"

Yoshi blushed but nodded.

Charles pointed to the female on stage whose nipples were now clearly visible under her bikini top. "Keiko, what about you?"

Keiko was too flustered to answer so Charles let him off the hook. "Why don't we get drinks for the ladies?" Servers would usually bring drinks to the table but it was an opportunity to display male gallantry.

By the time the two men returned to the table, the next act was just wrapping up. Charles gave Yoshi her drink.

Carmen smiled at Keiko as he carefully placed her drink in front of her. "Have you been to the disco?" she asked him.

He nodded and mimed a rock and roll dance. "You?" he asked.

"We prefer the piano bar," said Charles.

"Isn't that for swingers?" Keiko wanted to know.

"Sometimes," responded Carmen.

Yoshi looked back and forth between Charles and Carmen. "Are you swingers?"

Carmen patted her arm. "Yes. Are you?"

Keiko spluttered into his drink. "No."

"What's it like to swing?" asked Yoshi.

But the next act was loud, the band leader urging everyone to get up and dance. Carmen took Yoshi's hand and led her to the dance floor. The two women danced apart. As the song came to an end, Charles leaned over to Keiko. "Should we join the ladies?" he asked.

Keiko nodded and the two men made their way to the dance floor. The next number was a slower tune. Keiko headed for Yoshi, but Carmen subtly inserted herself and it was only polite for Keiko to ask her to dance. Charles ended up with Yoshi. The couples danced hand in hand, but their bodies did not touch. The song ended and the stage crew readied for an acrobatic number, the show's finale.

On the way back to their table, the ladies went first and Keiko pulled Charles back. "What's it like to swing?" he asked.

"It has to be what everyone feels comfortable with. It's important that you and Yoshi agree what you want to do."

At the end of the acrobatic show, the female performer ended up upside down with her legs spread. The male performer grabbed her by the waist, his head facing just above her outstretched legs, and he slowly turned around before lowering her to the floor.

Keiko and Yoshi were transfixed by the performers. Charles and Carmen watched their reactions.

When the show ended, the two young Japanese clapped enthusiastically, then took a long pull from their drinks.

"Why don't we go to the disco?" invited Carmen.

Keiko turned to Yoshi who nodded. "Sure," he said.

The music in the disco was too loud for conversation, but the beat was driving, making it easy to dance. The two couples danced separately at first but after a few songs switched partners. When it was time to switch again, Carmen maneuvered herself opposite Yoshi and the two women danced together, Charles moving behind Carmen, Keiko following suit behind Yoshi. The classic swingers sandwich. Carmen kissed Yoshi's lips and fondled her breasts, but avoided her nipples. Yoshi responded with a mixture of timidity and enthusiasm.

When the song changed, Carmen twirled Yoshi, exchanging places with the younger woman, so that now Keiko was behind her and Charles was behind Yoshi. Carmen pulled Keiko's hands around her waist bringing his crotch against her buttocks. She smiled when she felt something hard between them. Yoshi felt something similar between her buttocks and pulled her husband's hands upwards, pressing them to squeeze Carmen's breasts.

Carmen reached between Yoshi's thighs. Yoshi deepened the kiss and pushed her body forward, pressing Carmen's hands up against her panties.

The song ended with everyone out of breath. Carmen led them outside and they found a quiet spot around a small table. She turned to Yoshi. "Why don't you come back to our room?"

"I don't know," Keiko worried.

Carmen turned to him. "No one will be hurt. You can leave at any time."

Keiko turned to his wife. The movement of her head was subtle, but indicated interest. He turned to Charles. "What about birth control?"

Charles shrugged. "I've been snipped. Carmen is on the pill."

"Sexually transmitted disease?" Keiko wanted to know.

"We're clean," Carmen assured him. "We got tested just before we came down. Besides, we always use condoms."

Keiko was wavering. Yoshi gripped his hand.

Charles patted Keiko's shoulder. "Why don't you discuss it between just the two of you? Carmen and I will take a stroll down the beach."

"Charlie," protested Carmen when the younger couple was out of earshot, "they would have agreed."

Charles shrugged. "But only tentatively."

After a few minutes, Charles and Carmen turned around and glanced back towards the table. But Keiko and Yoshi were walking towards them. "We would like to," began Keiko.

"Swing with you," finished Yoshi.

"In your room, everyone together."

"All the way," finished Yoshi.

When Carmen shut the door to their room, she saw that Keiko and Yoshi were standing together, uncomfortable. "Should we start with a soft swap?" she asked.

"What's a soft swap?" asked Yoshi.

Carmen gave her a light kiss on the cheek. "Kissing and touching, but all clothes remain on."

Yoshi and Keiko relaxed noticeably. "Sure," they said in unison.

Charles took Yoshi by the hand and led her to the bench couch at the far end of the room. He would want to watch his wife lead Keiko further and further into the swing. He himself would remain one stage behind to ensure there were no masculine anxieties or territorial jealousies on the young man's part.

Carmen lay down on the bed and beckoned Keiko to join her. She pointed at her toes, then gradually moved her hands up her body before touching her lips. "Kiss me all over," she told him.

Keiko began at her ankles, then up the outside of her calves, then knees. Carmen spread her legs which directed his kisses up the inside of her thigh. Charles hugged Yoshi close and she hugged him back.

When Keiko tried to circle around her panties, Carmen reminded him, "*All* over."

Keiko kissed the top of Carmen's pubic bone. Yoshi squeezed Charles' thigh.

Keiko kissed up Carmen's belly and didn't try to avoid her breast. By the time he'd reached the top of her right breast, the outline of a nipple bud was clearly visible under Carmen's top.

Keiko kissed the nipple, pleased that it responded naturally beneath her thin bikini top. When Carmen moaned, he sucked the nipple into his mouth. He was doing it with another woman. And this one's nipples were even larger than his wife's. He felt his *inkei* strain to escape his briefs.

Keiko released Carmen's nipple and kissed above it, heading for her neck. But Carmen reminded him, "the other one too." Keiko blushed but gleefully complied. As he sucked her nipple, Carmen wiggled back and forth, loosening her top.

When he reached her lips, Carmen pulled him against her and he ended up flat against her body. Their kiss was sexual—whole body sexual—and Keiko pressed his midsection into her. Carmen felt his hardness arouse warmth within her own sex.

On the couch, Charles kissed Yoshi. It was a tentative kiss, he barely touched his lips to hers. But she responded enthusiastically and he held her close, licking just inside her mouth. He had stubble on his face. She smelt of Jasmine. He reached under her toga to touch her bra; she stroked his upper thighs. He reached under her sheet to free her bra, she moving to help him, her hand stroking upwards in the process.

Keiko came up for air. Charles broke off his own kiss and looked towards the bed. "Have you ever touched a woman?" he asked.

Yoshi shook her head. "No," she breathed.

Keiko rolled off Carmen and watched Charles help Yoshi to her feet. But he did not push her towards the bed. Carmen turned towards Yoshi. "You're beautiful," she told the smaller woman. Yoshi took a step forward.

Carmen could see that Yoshi was still uncertain. She pulled her bikini top down. "I'd like you to, but you don't have to if you don't want to," she told the younger woman.

But Yoshi shook her head, pushed Carmen back down onto the bed, and climbed atop her. Her kisses were even more passionate than her husband's had been. Charles motioned for Keiko to join him on the bed, each man kneeling on opposite sides of the women. They stroked up and down the moaning women beneath them, but avoided their genitals.

Charles rolled the women, Yoshi ending up beneath Carmen. Carmen raised herself on her knees and elbows, but maintained her kiss.

Charles removed his wife's bikini top and motioned for Keiko to touch her breasts. Keiko's caresses were at first tentative, but when he started to enjoy himself, Charles began to caress Yoshi's breasts. He smiled as his wife swallowed Yoshi's gasp.

Charles reached up under Yoshi's toga and caressed her thighs. Then, as he watched Keiko caresses the largest breasts he'd ever touched, Charles reached between Carmen's legs and pulled down on the thin straps holding her thong in place. With her cooperation, he soon had them off her legs. Charles led Keikos's hands between his wife's legs and watched his fingers enjoy his wife's pussy lips.

Carmen lifted herself to kneeling fully upright on the bed. Charles led Yoshi around her and the two of them began to flutter their hands up and down each other's bodies while kissing lightly.

Out of a corner of his eye, Charles watched Carmen strip Keiko's toga from his body. She sucked his cock into her mouth and his eyes bugged out.

Charles began to gently remove Yoshi's toga. Even though the evening was progressing wonderfully, he would remain one step behind his wife and Keiko, ensuring that no one was getting upset. It could be tricky with first-timers. He pulled the sheets from Yoshi's body and admired her sheer red panties.

But Charles needn't have worried; there was no problem at the other end of the bed. Carmen had unrolled a condom down Keiko's cock and she had laid down on the bed, her legs spread wide.

Charles took one of Yoshi's firm young breasts in each of his hands. He noted with satisfaction that her dark nipples were fully engorged. Just as Keiko slid himself into Carmen, he pulled Yoshi's panties off her ankles, marveling at her delicate pussy lips.

Charles kissed up and down Yoshi's perfect soft but firm body. There was no hint of hair anywhere.

Yoshi turned to see her husband's flushed face and saw that he was close to his climax. She turned back to Charles. "Hurry. Please."

Charles glanced at Keiko. He was too far gone to pull back. Charles quickly unrolled a condom over his erection and pressed the tip of his cock against Yoshi's pussy. He slid right in. She bucked herself against him, urging him to come as quickly as he could.

"Please!" begged Yoshi. "I don't want him to see me come."

Charles altered his hips slightly sideways and continued his long, firm thrusts. Yoshi was enjoying his efforts, but her arousal had not noticeably accelerated. He shifted himself to the other side of her head and was rewarded with a gasp from below.

"Yes!" whispered Yoshi so that her husband would not hear. "Harder! Faster!" Charles was larger than her husband and his thrusts touched areas her husband's *inkei* missed. She wanted the whole experience. She wanted a memory, a memory to savor forever. Charles was moving just right and she moaned her encouragement.

But beside her, she could feel her husband's breathing quicken.

"Slow him down, she whispered frantically." She had no idea how Charles might accomplish this, but he was her only hope.

"Carmen!" she heard him pant above her. "Let him see your ass!"

Yoshi felt the bed jiggle beside them. Keiko's *inkei* had popped out. She didn't know how she knew this. But he was heaving deep breaths into his lungs. Then he was lying beside her. She turned and smiled at him. He smiled back. What had Charles meant, "Let him see your ass"? Then she caught sight of Carmen climbing atop Keiko. Keiko was looking up and Yoshi followed his gaze. There, in the mirror, was Carmen's ass. And better yet, there was Charles' ass pumping himself into her.

Yoshi's eyes were transfixed on Charles' glutes, contracting and releasing. But the rest of her consciousness was inside her *chitsu* where Charles was stimulating her in ways she'd never been stimulated before. She felt heat and tightness build each time Charles clenched his glutes. Then without being aware of it, she was floating, flying, her wings flapping each time Charles clenched himself inside her.

Suddenly, Yoshi felt her whole body snap straight as a board, fastening her to the mattress as her orgasm shot up her spine, swirled inside her *chitsu,* then tickled down her legs. Wave after wave of desire and pleasure and gratification rolled up and down her body. She could feel her husband approaching his climax beside her. But she had climbed the mountain first and she would have enough time to shut her eyes and float gently back down.

At the last minute, Keiko tried to stop his orgasm. He was being unfaithful to Yoshi. But the white woman with her fantastic round breasts and her strong firm *chitsu* was too much and he spurted inside the latex tube encasing his *inkei.* At the first contraction on the base of his *inkei,* he glanced sideways at his wife, at her wide, pure smile. And he smiled too. They had done it together. Neither was being unfaithful. The next contraction tickled up his spine, as he relaxed into the joy of the moment. Squeezing his last drop tickled the soles of his feet.

Charles looked over at Carmen and they smiled the smile of conquest together. Now it was time for their own climaxes. Charles angled his cock straight into Yoshi. He grabbed her ass and mashed himself as far inside her cunt as he could manage. Then he ferociously impaled her, slamming himself in and out with reckless abandon. His cock surged pulses of power into the small Asian woman beneath him. Carmen reveled in all three of the previous orgasms as she slowly caressed her cunt up and down Keiko's cock. Her own orgasm lacked the fury of those which had gone before, but was deeper and hotter, undulating up her spine, then down her legs. As her climax receded, it radiated warmth out in every direction, hottest at the center of her cunt, most delicious in her cheeks, most delightful in her toes.

Chapter 6

Nathan and Sophie Weiland were returning to Hedonism after a long absence and were eager to see what changes the new management had made to the resort. They'd visited twice in the nineties when the resort was in its heyday, then once in the late 2009 when the former owners were allowing it to slide into decline.

The first thing they noticed was that the lovely ceramic mural filled with flowers and a smiling hippie in front of the sit-down reception desk had been replaced by art-deco polka dots and a stand-up marble countertop. Their hearts sank; surely this was a step backwards. But it was lunchtime and they were encouraged to eat before performing the check-in process—at least the welcoming hospitality hadn't changed!

Bellies filled, Nathan and Sophie were invited to sit in one of the comfortable lounge chairs while the receptionist flitted back and forth with the necessary documents to check them in.

"Is it my imagination, or are the staff happier this time?" Sophie asked.

Nathan nodded. "And more attentive."

The receptionist came back with their keycards. "Mr. and Mrs. Weiland, your bags are already in your room. Would you like someone to accompany you to show—"

Sophie shook her head and smiled. "No, but thank you. We'd like to take a lazy stroll first."

The receptionist smiled, nodded, and left them.

The Weilands walked back towards and through the dining area. Outside, there was a bright blue swimming pool in which several couples were playing volleyball. At the far end was a stairway tower which they climbed.

"This was closed the last time we were here," remarked Nathan.

By the time they ascended the last stair, they were fifty feet above ground level. The Weilands walked halfway along the walkway, then paused and stared out towards the ocean in quiet contemplation. They were in their sixties, she a few years older than he. Sophie stood five-feet five inches tall; she had short red hair and green eyes. Her body was a bit overweight, however this was balanced by her large breasts. Nathan was six feet tall, thin, but not particularly fit. His cheeks were a bit sunk in. Atop his head, grey had long since taken over brown. Their skin was pasty white.

Staring down, they saw billiard tables—both on land and in a shallow pool. All around them, coconut trees swayed in the wind.

Nathan pointed to an outdoor bed. "That's new," he remarked.

As they walked along the water, they came to the edge of the nude beach and its sign, "No Clothing Allowed". She squeezed his arm, "Remember how shocked we were, the first time?" she asked.

He turned and gave her a kiss. "And then how we jumped in head first, strutting our bods *au natural* for all to see—"

"Making out in the disco—"

"You made me cream my pants and we had to rush back to our room."

"And then the swinging."

"What was the name of the first couple?" he asked.

"Leroy and Sandy."

"You were hot to trot to see if it was true what they said about black men."

"And you wanted to see if her pussy tasted of brown sugar."

They laughed and kissed. A long, lingering kiss. A kiss that provoked stirrings in their loins. They were halfway down the nude beach so they quickly stripped, deposited their clothes on a lounge chair, and strode into the water. They looked around at all the naked bodies on full display along the beach. But no one seemed to be watching them.

"Do you think anyone would still be interested in us?" she asked.

"They'd be foolish not to be." He turned her back to his chest and cupped her full breasts in his hands, lifting them gently up, feeling her nipples engorge between his fingers.

"Nathan!" she objected, but there was almost as much encouragement as protest in her voice.

The strains of children—pregnancy and childbirth along with the struggles and stresses of raising two independent and intelligent teenagers—had aged her body. What was once firm, now tended to sag. But she was still the most beautiful woman in the world. Especially when a smile brightened her lively green eyes.

After having absorbed enough sunshine for one day, they gathered their clothes and headed towards their room.

Nathan was about to slide his keycard into the lock on the door to their room when Sophie's hand on his wrist stopped him. He had wrapped a towel from the beach stand around his waist. Her towel was tied at her shoulder and waist, all but covering her body. Their clothes and shoes were gathered in another towel that he was holding in his left hand. He stood up and turned to her.

"I don't want to go in until we've talked," she told him. Her voice was firm. She was standing straight, her weight centered.

"It was my fault." He looked into her eyes, trying to gauge whether his apology was sufficient.

"Are you saying that because you're sorry, or because you know I won't be the first to apologize?"

"Both." That was fair, and they both knew it. His honesty melted her stance, but only slightly. They had had a knockdown argument last night, just before their departure for Jamaica.

"You told me that I cared more about the shop than I did about you, that I didn't really love you anymore." She managed a lingerie shop, her pride and joy.

"That's how I felt." He made a vague circular motion with right hand, flipping the keycard back and forth as if it was an airliner's wing flap.

"Maybe if you helped out more around the house, I'd have more time for you."

"Sophie—"

"And you made me pack half the house. We're only here for a week!"

"I have to concentrate on my programming if we're going to send Steve to Yale." He was still back on the domestic chore split. His computer programming business brought in the bulk of their household's income.

She exhaled, suddenly sad. "Nathan, why are we fighting?"

"Because we care about each other."

She nodded, reached for his right hand and aimed the keycard at the slot in the lock.

Inside, she unpacked their clothing while he checked their email accounts, grateful that WiFi was now free at the resort. Then after a quick shower together—a shower which came within a hair's breadth of turning into a quickie, they returned to the nude beach. There, they lathered on sunscreen and lounged on beach chairs, alternating their attention between the vista of the ocean before them, the inshore where nude couples were bathing or frolicking, and the wide variety naked couples walking back and forth just in front of them. Every so often they sampled their plates of chicken and french fries, which were still steaming hot from the beachside grill.

"Everyone looks so young," remarked Sophie.

"Youth is a state of mind." He stuffed his mouth full of french fries.

"I'm serious."

"So am I." He turned to her, attempting to gauge her mood.

"We're not like them." She pointed to a young couple in the water. Their hips were covered by the ocean but he was bending down to suck on her nipples.

"We could be."

She slapped his thigh. "Maybe next year, we should go to Sandals."

"Safe and staid and *boring* Sandals?"

"What does Hedonism have that Sandals doesn't?" The young couple was kissing. Although the pair's hips were underwater, their characteristic motions left little doubt as to what was going on.

"That," he responded.

"For *us*."

"Want to give it a try?"

"Nathan!" She blushed. But she also smiled, remembering long ago when it was her in the water, rocking back and forth against *his* hips, feeling *him* plunge in and out of *her* as the waves lapped against her back.

He smiled and kissed her forehead. "Maybe that isn't for us now, but there's still something special about the electric erotic atmosphere at Hedo." He felt blood begin to swell his penis.

"There isn't anything new for us here," she continued. "Ganja is freely, and legally, available back home."

He spotted Keiko and Yoshi approaching in the distance. "I've always had a thing for Asian women."

She followed his line of sight, sighed, put her plate aside, and propped herself up. "Is that what you want?"

"I want you."

"But if you could have both?" Computer code might be binary, but life wasn't.

He looked at his wife. She would always do what he wanted. But now it was his turn. "I want you," he repeated. "But I want my fantasies as well."

Sophie reached over and kissed him, her left hand patting below the waist. She smiled as something started to bulge beneath her hand. She broke of the kiss, stood and smiled in the direction of the young Asian couple. If he wanted fantasies, she would be happy to oblige.

Sophie waved at the young couple. When they turned her way, she nodded and smiled again. Keiko and Yoshi began to walk over. Yoshi pushed her long black hair behind her shoulders, unintentionally giving Nathan a better view of her pert little breasts. Nathan began to rise, but Sophie pushed him back down to his lounge chair and resumed her own seat. Her choreography resulted in the younger couple ending up in the space between their two chairs.

Sophie reached out and briefly squeezed Yoshi's hand. "My husband says that you're beautiful," she told her.

Yoshi blushed but her effort to turn away brought her face to face with Nathan's smile.

Behind her, Yoshi heard Sophie address her husband. "I'm Sophie and that's Nathan."

"Keiko and Yoshi."

"Hi, Yoshi," said Nathan. "Have you been enjoying your stay at Hedo?"

She nodded.

"How was toga night?"

"You're so big," they heard Sophie say on the other side of Keiko's back. "And getting bigger." There was the creak of a chair being adjusted. "Here let me move so that you can get a better look at me."

Yoshi's blush deepened and she fought not to turn around.

"How am I," asked Nathan in a low, conspiratorial voice. "Am I big too?" He reached down and adjusted himself to accommodate the effects of blood flowing into his penis.

"You're growing," whispered Yoshi.

"Have you ever seen a man grow before? Other than your husband?" he whispered back.

She nodded. "Last night?"

"How was that?"

"We went swinging."

"Did you enjoy yourself?"

She nodded, but cast her eyes down.

"Let me see you," he whispered.

She kept her eyes downcast but lifted her foot onto the chair beside him. When she touched his leg, she tried to pull her foot back. But he held it close and stroked its soft underside. She gasped.

"You're beautiful," he whispered.

Yoshi opened her eyes and followed his gaze to her crotch.

"Show me," he whispered.

Yoshi reached down and parted her pussy lips. She bit her lip at the reaction between his legs.

"Are you going to swing again?" they heard Sophie's voice from the other side of Keiko's back.

Yoshi quickly replanted her foot on the sand as she saw her husband turning. His penis was almost parallel to the sand on which Yoshi's feet were fidgeting.

"May be," stuttered Keiko.

Sophie stood up and wrapped a towel around herself, tapping Nathan's shoulder for him to follow suit. "Good!" responded Sophie. "We have an appointment for a massage at the spa. Maybe we'll catch up with you later."

As Sophie and Nathan ambled off, Sophie smiled to herself as she tried to figure out whose expression had been more crestfallen, Keiko's or Nathan's. She grinned at the awkward way both men were walking.

That night, the dress theme was leather and lingerie. For dinner, Sophie had worn a black lace bodysuit with only a shorter-than-short red leather miniskirt to cover her midsection. Her breasts bounced freely, their nipples struggling to poke through the lace. Nathan was nude to the waist and below he was wearing only a skimpy pair of tight pleather shorts. Most of the women were dressed sexily, but only a few of the men. Sophie held tight to Nathan's arm, proud at how adventurous he was.

After a hearty meal at Pastafari, the resort's full-service Italian restaurant, Nathan shut his eyes and leaned back to let his food digest. He felt something between his legs and reached down to verify that it was his wife's foot.

"So, what should we do *tonight*?" purred Sophie.

"Dessert."

"Dessert?!?"

"They have custard and pudding. Both with whipped cream."

"Nate, that's adult *entertainment*," she teased, "not dessert." But she knew what he had in mind. Her nipples engorged at the thought of cold custard followed by his mouth sucking the custard off, then licking to make sure he'd got every last drop.

He opened one eye, saw her grinning back at him, and shut his eye. He felt a smile slowly spread across his face at the thought of Sophie spreading pudding up and down his shaft.

The evening's show had a vaguely BDSM tone with a small woman pressing a much larger and muscular man down to the floor with her high heels. Partway through, Keiko and Yoshi entered. She was tied kinbaku-style with crisscrossing leather lacings and being led by a leash wielded by Keiko.

Sophie was now sitting next to Nathan and she squeezed his hand to direct his attention to the young Japanese couple. "Nate," she whispered.

Nathan opened his eyes and was suddenly uncomfortable in his tight pleather shorts. Asian sex. Kinky *Japanese* sex! "Is that what you want?" he whispered back.

"I want what you want."

That was one of the ruts they had fallen into. Always suppressing themselves for the other, not saying what they really wanted.

"Imagine I have you tied up tight," he whispered. "Your joints are uncomfortable. I've put water on the ropes and they're shrinking. You want to cry out in pain, but your pride is stopping you. The only way to escape the ropes is to answer my question. Truthfully. What do you want?" He reached around and pinched one of her nipples. "Here and now. What do you want?"

"Dessert," gasped Sophie.

Back in their room, Nathan pointed to their bed. "Lie down, spread-eagled."

She spread her arms at right-angles from her body and spread her legs. But she didn't resist when he pressed her legs together and slid her miniskirt off along with her sandals. Beneath her black lace bodysuit, she had only a thin white thong. As he lifted her legs apart, he caught a glimpse of tanned skin under the white satin. He removed his shorts and felt himself spring free, at last relieving the discomfort between his legs. Sophie looked over and smiled at the effect the evening's proceedings were having on her husband.

"Shut your eyes," he told her, holding up a cup of custard.

She shook her head. He'd been careful to let her see the custard and had let her carry two cups of chocolate pudding. But he'd hid the cup of soft ice cream from her. He held it out now and let a drop of condensation fall on her belly.

"Nathan!" she exclaimed, protesting the cold.

He tipped the cup slightly. "Shut your eyes or I'll pour the whole thing right onto your belly."

Sophie shut her eyes and made a show of scrunching them tight.

He dipped his finger into the ice cream and placed a small dab on her nipple. She shivered. He placed a large dollop on the second nipple.

Sophie shuddered. "Nate!" she screamed.

He sucked the larger dollop off first and she calmed. He licked all around the nipple, feeling it warm on his tongue, hard between his lips. He pinched the ice cream off her other nipple and she moaned.

The cold was torture, especially on her sensitive nipples and Sophie struggled to relax and take deep breaths. But the cold being sucked off her nipples was arousing her, almost against her will.

Nathan caressed her belly and felt her whole abdomen tense. He smiled at her preparation for more ice cream. But instead he placed a dollop of whipped cream into her belly button. He sucked and licked. She tensed first her right side to avoid the tickle, then her left. Then he blew a raspberry into her tummy and she writhed with the force of the tickle shooting up and down her body.

"Nate!" she screamed.

When she was lying still again, he poured chocolate pudding

under her thong smiling as it changed color. Above, he kissed across her breasts and flicked the tip of his tongue around her nipples. Below, he pressed her thong, and the gooey pudding, inside, into her pussy. There was nothing sexier than feeling his wife's pussy lips warm and engorge. Then he slipped his fingers under her thong and used the lubrication of the pudding to slide them rapidly up and down her sex.

The gooiness initially robbed her of almost all feeling, but as the pudding dissipated, her responsiveness returned, dampness and heat filling her sex. She relaxed into the strokes of Nate's fingers, feeling her arousal build.

When the pudding was almost entirely dispersed, he rose over her and mounted her, his penis sliding easily inside.

Beneath him, she opened her eyes, reached up and pinched his nipples. "Dessert is for eating," she reminded him. "Your turn to lie on your back."

Nathan reluctantly withdrew and felt cool air replace the wet heat he'd been experiencing below. He turned and laid on his back.

Sophie knelt over his torso, facing down towards his hips, a knee on either side. He felt a full bowl of custard being poured over his pubic bone and sexual organs. Then her tongue lapping it up. When she bent to reach below, she lifted her hips up and he caught sight of her pussy peeking out from under her thong.

Then Sophie raised herself upright, adjusted her thong and poured more custard inside. She leaned back pressing the thong against his lips. The custard was cold, but his mouth was hot. She channeled the sensations into her hands stroking up and down his penis.

First the taste of custard, rich and sweet, then the feel of satin and lycra on his tongue. When he sucked hard, he felt her buckle atop him and her breasts momentarily touch his skin. Then her mouth enveloped his cock. And sucked! When Nathan recovered, he reached up to push her thong aside. When he licked his tongue up and down her sex, he felt her jiggle and almost lose her balance. He waited until she lifted her head off his cock, then he flicked his tongue against her clit. This time Sophie did lose her balance and she fell down beside him.

Nathan turned towards her, but Sophie pushed him back down. She dabbed whipping cream on each of her nipples, then bent them to his mouth, allowing him only a quick flick of his tongue on each nipple.

Then she readjusted her thong and poured chocolate pudding down it.

This time when she climbed atop his head, she faced away from him and steadied herself by holding onto the wood inlaid into the wall at the head of the bed.

"If you want to breathe, you'd better make me come," she teased.

She felt her legs slide over his cheeks and his mouth kiss her gently through her thong. His second kiss sucked so much pudding out from her sex she almost swooned. She held tightly to the curve of the wood. Her threat of suffocation was empty, she was already on the cusp of climax. His tongue lapped the length of her thong and she felt wetness inside replace the sticky gooey feel of the pudding.

Nathan sucked pudding into his mouth. His wife tasted good, with or without pudding. But tonight he needed the extra calories! Chocolate for sweet, pussy for sharp and salt. He was in heaven. Even though she wasn't touching him, he could feel his penis throbbing.

She felt his fingers move to push her thong aside and she lifted herself slightly to assist. Then his tongue lapped upward from the bottom of her sex and she lost the ability to hold herself upright without resting on his face. She sensed her climax begin to tug downwards on her belly. Dimly she felt his fingers squeeze her nipples, sending jolts downward into the storm roiling below. Sophie rocked herself against him, urging him to press harder inside her.

Then—then he sucked! Her clit, he sucked it into his mouth! And she had to stop moving. He sucked it in and out, gently, but firmly. As if giving it a soft and tender blow job. She was counting down. She could feel it beginning. Six. Five. Four. She took the deepest breath she could manage. Three. Two! *One*! Detonated the explosion and she lost consciousness.

Nathan felt his wife's climax as a series of contractions on the outside of her sex. He wished he'd had his fingers inside her so that he could feel their full force.

Sophie emerged from the blinding whiteness, from the waves of white-hot heat smashing against her. "Fuck!" she screamed. Below, Nathan enveloped her sex with his mouth, sucked and thrust his tongue inside her. She almost fell off him again as a jolt of electricity whipped up her spine. Each tongue thrust clenched her tight in blissful agony.

Each time his tongue withdrew, it left behind soft warmth. Sophie felt her orgasm recede in sparkles of delight. But Nate didn't stop. His tongue was tracing zigzag zipper patterns up her pussy lips and she knew that he would quickly bring her to a second climax, one which would pry her hands loose from the inlaid wood. She lifted herself up and flopped onto her back beside him.

As Nate turned towards her, she saw him smiling in triumph, she saw his cock quivering with desire. By rights she should give him a handjob with the remaining pudding. But she wasn't sure she had the strength. Besides she should let him plow himself inside her, let him feel raw male dominance.

"Fuck me!" she urged.

Nathan didn't need a second invitation and quickly rolled atop her and slammed himself inside. Sophie was too lubricated to feel much down below. But in her heart, she gloried in her husband's lust, gloried in him shuddering to a stop at the crest of the hill, gloried at him spasming his life force into her.

Chapter 7

The morning had begun with Bassim waking up in the glow of his wife cuddling her warm body next to his. Last night they had stayed in, spending a quiet evening reading, then falling asleep in each other's arms.

The night before had been quite a different story. They had spent more than an hour trying to adjust their sheets into makeshift togas. But, try as they might, they never managed to pull off the ancient European outfit against their dark South East Asian skin. But they had had fun, especially when they had found a dark corner in the Romping Room where Damini had slipped under his sheet to administer oral sex. They had scampered back to their room, where he had returned the favor. She had purred in his arms as they had fallen asleep.

This morning, their bodies still entwined, they had read for an hour before strolling to the dining room to sample the sumptuous buffet. Later, they had let the warm glow of a full breakfast dissipate while wandering along the water's edge. On the dock they kept pace with the translucent fish swimming alongside, watching sunlight sparkle within their long thin bodies. When the morning snorkelers began to gather, they'd scurried back to their rooms, donned swimsuits, checked-out masks and snorkels and joined the fishes *inside* the water. Bassim saw grunts, an eel and two puffer fish. But the beauty of the sea creatures faded next to that of his wife as she dove beneath the waves.

After lunch—jerk chicken was even better than the curried variety—Bassim and Damini had found a quiet spot in the shade where they had pledged their undying loyalty to each other. He had forgiven her affair, letting his anger fly off with the wind. She had saluted his willingness to be more adventurous.

In that spirit of mutual joy and reconciliation, they had dropped into the resort's gift shop to supplement their wardrobes for that evening's theme: Bare As You Dare Glow Pool Party. She had purchased a lime green miniskirt to accompany her lace bra and panties set. For him, she had selected a pair of white form-fitting lycra shorts. "What should I wear on top?" he'd asked.

Damini has shaken her head and caressed his nipples. "Nothing."

Bassim had shaken his hips seductively, causing his belly to ripple.

They'd laughed and she'd felt a tingle inside her sex as she contemplated caressing his hardness through the thin material while they danced among other scantily clad couples.

The aura of rekindled love continued as they dressed for dinner: his eyes devoured the bright lingerie highlighting her curvaceous and fit body. She basked in the attention of her tall, handsome, and charismatic husband, eager to run her fingers over his soft parts, eager to feel them become his hard parts.

The glow of her happiness continued at dinner as she felt the eyes of virile young men devouring her. But she was sad that none of the women even glanced at her husband as his girth jiggled around the dessert table. She shook her head; they didn't know what she had; Bassim was hers—kind, attentive and loyal.

Damini finished her main course and was about to join her husband at the dessert table. However, when she stood, a familiar face crossed her path, startling her.

"Eric!" she blurted.

Bassim looked up at his wife and at the man standing between them. Eric's muscles rippled around the straps of his tank-top.

"Damini?" Eric recovered quickly and looked for a place to hide.

Bassim ambled over. "Is this Eric Agnarson?" he asked, his voice low, accusatory. Damini tried her best to swallow her excitement at Eric's sudden appearance.

A woman joined them, looking back and forth between the South East Asian couple, but mostly at Damini. "Eric?" she asked.

"He is neither skinny nor short," Bassim accused. Eric was nothing at all like his wife's description.

Eric pointed his wife towards Damini, "Claire, you remember Damini Agarwal, our real estate agent?"

"Sex included," Bassim added.

Claire was dumbfounded. She looked to her husband for an explanation. "Eric?"

"They're having an affair," clarified Bassim. "Right under our noses." His voice was no longer low; now it filled the room. The surrounding tables had fallen silent as their occupants watched the drama in front of them.

"How many times did you have sex with him?" demanded Bassim.

"Bassim!" wailed Damini.

"How many!" yelled Bassim.

"Eric?" pleaded Claire. "What's going on?"

Eric tried to move his wife to one side. "It was one time. It's over."

But Claire refused to budge. "And yet here we are. Is this what you had in mind when you promised a *special* vacation?!?"

Eric had no answer and his wife stomped off.

"Our marriage is over," Bassim told his wife. Then he waved his arm across the entire dining room. "Over!" He strode off, head held high in full Brahmin dignity.

Eric looked back and forth between Damini and his wife's retreating back. He dashed after his wife.

Damini slumped down into her chair, her head in her hands. A single, solitary tear wandered down her cheek. People swirled around her, sitting, getting up, eating, drinking, leaving. However Damini was only dimly aware of them. She was alone, completely cut off. But she was only a little sad. When she realized that she was only a *little* sad, she wondered why she wasn't more dejected, more desolate. But then she realized that a weight had been lifted from her shoulders, the weight of all the lies she'd been telling herself about how happy she was being married to Bassim.

Damini rose from her seat and walked out in a fog. She only became aware of her location when a cool ocean breeze hit her face. She took a deep breath and decided to go for a walk along the beach.

Meanwhile, Bassim's path of exit had taken him away from his room and, by the time he'd circled back towards his room, Eric and Claire were blocking the trail ahead. Eric was in his late thirties, Claire a few years older. They were both white, their bodies thin from long-distant running. He was muscular and young and virile. She was full of energy, lithe, feline. They were shouting at each other, often talking at the same time. Bassim caught only the odd word or phrase: 'lawyer', 'mother', 'sell house', 'children'. Eric paused to take a breath and Bassim heard her voice, clear as a bell, "Fuck you, you little shit!"

Claire pushed her husband, he stumbled, then walked around her and away.

Claire spotted Bassim and walked purposefully towards him. Bassim had nowhere to go so he stood by the side of the path, hoping that she would walk on by. Instead, she walked right up to him. "It's time for my evening run, but I'd rather have sex with you," she announced.

Bassim looked at the passion in her cobalt blue eyes and exotic blonde hair. She was wearing neon pink: tight spandex hot-pant shorts and a tight tank-top under which he could see her nipples. Not at all like Damini. Not like the woman who— Payback was payback. Besides, he did not know when next he would be provided with an opportunity for sex. Bassim nodded.

She smiled. "Good. Since it's in place of my evening run, I'll do all the work."

Bassim wasn't quite sure what that meant, but he nodded.

Claire led him to her room where she secured the door from the inside. He stood still, uncertain what to do next. But her hand squeezing him through the soft thin material covering his crotch left no doubt what she wanted. And his own physical reaction convinced him that it was what he wanted as well. His hands drifted up her torso—it was skinny and hard, until they reached her breasts. Her breasts were firm and soft all at the same time, little mounds atop her chest. But her nipples were prominent and hard, leaving no doubt that they belonged to a fully matured woman.

She kissed his lips, flicking her tongue just inside his mouth. She had no taste, but she did have heat and texture. He kissed her back and felt her body press against his with unabashed passion. When they came up for air, she kissed down the length of his body and slid his lycra shorts to the floor.

Her lips on the tip of his penis were even hotter than they'd been on his own lips. Warm wetness slid down his entire length while fingers fluttered over his wrinkled egg sack. He wobbled but managed to remain standing. Only when she'd slid up and down the third time did he remember to breathe.

She stood and led him to the bed, pushing him onto his back. Somehow she'd removed her clothing. Nude, she was even more pencil-thin, the only break from her smooth tube were tufts of blonde hair atop her head and between her hips. She knelt astride one of his legs, one hand cupping his balls, the other grasping his shaft.

The door rattled and Eric called out. They ignored him.

Claire slowly stroked around Bassim's balls, up his shaft and then back down, completing circuit after circuit. "I want you to lie on your back," she told him. "I want to do all the work. I want you to remain still. Can you do that for me?"

"Yes."

"And I don't want talk."

Bassim nodded.

She climbed up his body, staring into the distance over his head, spread her legs, reached below and guided him into her. Her sex was as hot as her mouth had been, not as sharp, but more enveloping. She ground their pubic bones together, barely thrusting in and out. He longed to turn her beneath him, to plunge himself into her, long fast strokes, but he had promised to remain on his back. He reached up for her breasts, but she pushed his hands away.

Bassim stared up at her. She was the only woman who'd ever taken him like this. The only woman he'd been with since he married his wife many, many years ago. There was a flush up the middle of her chest. Her breasts had shrunk but her nipples were long and hard, making off-kilter circles as she ground her sex into his pubic bone. She was staring off into the distance somewhere over his head.

Then she glanced down at him. Her lips were smiling, but her eyes were ferocious. She lifted her hips up, then slowly lowered herself down the length of his shaft. He felt her slide over each and every indentation, he felt her hair tickle. She took a deep breath and he followed suit, bracing for what was to come next.

Claire raised herself half way, then lowered herself back down, but only two inches. She was rubbing his most sensitive part, just under the head of his penis. She did this twice more, slowly, locking her eyes on his. Then her thrusts sped up. It was hot, she had him in her control. He couldn't have moved even if he'd wanted to. He felt his belly tighten as she dragged him to the edge of the plateau. But now she was moving so quickly that the sensations on his shaft were beginning to dull.

Claire sensed that he was aroused but that he was in her thrall:

worshiping but unable to escape into ecstasy. She could run her marathon and he wouldn't be able to come until she'd made it to the finish line. She felt a trickle of sweat dribble down her spine as she rounded the half-way marker.

Claire lowered herself all the way down his shaft, rotated against his pubic bone, then lifted herself almost all the way off of him. Three more times to be sure she had the distance right, then she picked up the pace.

Bassim stared up into the cobalt eyes devouring him. Her lengthened strokes had dragged him halfway into the plateau, but now she had anchored him there with the rapidity of her strokes, a rapidity which dulled the sensation. Only a trained athlete would have been capable of that. Sweat was pouring off her body. He reached for her breasts. The ferocity in her eyes warned him against this trespass but his hands on her nipples, slipping and sliding with her sweat was worth the rebuke. Except suddenly his hands were held fast to her breasts, as if attached by a magnet. Her eyes gloated. She used his hands as a fulcrum and increased the power and speed of her thrusting hips.

Claire could sense the finish line approaching. Soon she would have her vengeance! She shut her eyes and slowed her thrusts. She brushed his hands away and rested her own against his chest. He too was approaching climax. She stumbled forward, felt a flutter inside her sex, felt him dribble down her thighs, felt heat roar up her spine, then vibrate, deep hard vibrations, at her core. She'd had better orgasms, but none so satisfying.

By the time Damini got back to the disco, dancing was starting. She entered and spotted the young Asian couple she and her husband had watched in the Romping Room. They were wearing one of the multi-colored neon outfits she'd seen in the gift shop, the type of thing she hadn't even dared suggest to Bassim.

Keiko's outfit began with a skin-tight top which ended just above his belly button. Bands of bright orange, lime-green, pink, white, and light blue went up and down his shirt, each color separated by a band of black. His bottom was the size of a bikini with bands of identical colors. Yoshi was wearing a similar outfit, but hers was a dress and extended barely below her hips. Damini stood at the edge of the dancers watching the young Japanese couple sway to a Bob Marley standard.

Meanwhile, Bassim, having left a good-bye note for his wife, was wheeling his bag to the front desk and the taxi waiting to take him back to the safety of home. Thankfully, there was enough width to the pathways that he was able to skirt around Eric and Claire who had resumed their angry argument. As best Bassim could discern, Eric had packed his bag and she was daring him to leave the resort. Bassim picked up his pace; he did not want to have to share a taxi with his wife's lover.

At a gap in the music, Yoshi pointed back and forth between Damini's skirt and the lime-green in her own dress and waved her over. The song had a driving beat and they danced apart, at first Damini with Keiko, then Damini with Yoshi, then the trio together in a triangle. When the music slowed, all three danced close to each other. Damini's body was barely touching theirs, but the effect was electric nonetheless. Then she felt the other woman slide behind her and press her firmly against her husband.

The trio had moved towards the center of the disco. All around her, Damini saw other dancers rubbing against each other, their hands fondling breasts and genitals. Keiko's hands squeezed her bra. Yoshi reached around her midsection and stroked up and down the front of her panties. Damini felt a warm rod press against her belly and she stepped aside to escape it. But Yoshi held her close and kissed her. Then the Japanese woman pulled her hair over her shoulder, knelt down, and took her husband's penis into her mouth.

As the song ended, Yoshi stood and attempted to shield her husband's *inkei* from view. "We should get a room," she whispered to Damini.

"I—" stuttered Damini.

"Our room?" queried Yoshi.

All three nodded.

As they walked along the beach towards their room, the two women giggled as they kept themselves in position to block anyone from seeing Keiko's erection.

Once through the sliding doors, clothes were quickly removed. A moment of hesitation. Then Yoshi pushed the brown-skinned woman into her husband's arms. Damini felt his lips, small and delicate, then his tongue, even smaller and more delicate. Below, fingers probed her pussy and she suddenly realized how aroused she was. As he turned her back towards his wife, Damini sensed something warm on her thigh, then lips even smaller and more delicate on hers.

The young couple laid the darker woman onto the bed between them and admired her voluptuous curves while gently running their hands up and down her body. Keiko squeezed her breasts. He had never touched a dark-skinned woman before, nor felt such naturally large mammaries in his hands and his penis twitched with enjoyment.

Yoshi slid down to kneel on the floor, her head between Damini's legs. The darker woman's sex was a pungent mix of jasmine and curry. She lapped at it voraciously, a smile tickling her lips as she heard a gasp above her.

Damini tried to fondle and kiss Keiko's erection but he was too far out of position for her to be able to have much effect. Besides, he seemed content to fondle her breasts. Below, Yoshi's tongue triggered sensations she never knew were possible. She was swinging. She was having a threesome. Even in her dreams, it was never this *exhilarating*!

Yoshi climbed up the bed, kissing along Damini's body as she went until she was pressed against the length of the darker woman. She kissed her and held her close.

Damini felt hands caress her pubic hair, then lower, fingers dipping inside. Yoshi's breath against her ear sent shivers down her spine. "Would you like to taste me?" asked Yoshi.

The shivers were unbearable and all Damini could do was nod.

There was shuffling as Yoshi and Keiko adjusted positions. Keiko was half kneeling, half standing at the end of the bed. Yoshi pulled Damini down towards her husband. Damini spread her legs. "Please," she mumbled and he slid himself between her pussy lips. Damini felt the twitch of a mini-climax inside her.

Yoshi was above her head and Damini felt her come forward, kneeling over her face, facing her husband. Damini stared hungrily up at the subtly pink insides of Yoshi's sex, at the pussy lips so fine as to be almost invisible, but so elegant nonetheless. And then this small slice of heaven was lowered down onto her lips and all Damini could see was the outline of Yoshi's bum.

Yoshi tasted of cherry blossoms with just a hint of oysters. Her skin was soft and delicate beyond description. Damini felt another climax down below as Keiko thrust steadily in and out. She lapped up and down Yoshi's sex, feeling it warming, feeling the fine pussy lips harden against her tongue.

Damini wanted the moment to last forever, to last as long as she'd been hungering for it. But Keiko's thrusts were wrenching control from her grasp and Yoshi's fingers stroking the sides of her clit pulled her towards the warm wet center. Yoshi was rocking her pale yellow skin back and forth along her tongue. Worse, the small woman above her was lifting herself up and down, controlling her breathing, forcing her to concentrate on sucking air into her lungs, distracting her from forestalling her climax.

Keiko was the first to yell. Yoshi screamed and Damini could feel the small woman's pussy lips flutter spasmodically against her tongue. The white hot explosion between her own legs pulled her down, as if she was on a plunging rollercoaster, and all Damini could do was surrender to the wrenching climax as she plummeted headlong into the abyss. The rollercoaster roared and flew up and over the apex, her spasms rocking the car as if to throw it off the track. She held on as tightly as she could until the spasms gently receded, each a spasm a click along the track.

Chapter 8

At the Save-the-Reef demonstration, the crowd of protesters had largely evaporated. All that remained were the two cops lounging against the coconut tree, Christopher Lang, Diane Chumak, and another couple.

But there were two newcomers: a pair of Jamaican lawyers trying to work out a settlement. The one in the grey suit represented the interests of the artificial reef, the one in the light blue suit, those of the developer. Somehow, despite the heat, they looked comfortable in their attire. Chris and Diane were standing within earshot of the lawyers, trying to understand the give and take of the negotiation. The other couple, a pair of young Canadians, stood to one side, waiting for the shuttle to take them back to their resort.

Diane pulled Chris aside. "What are you going to do once this is all over?" she asked.

"There's a non-government organization building houses in Haiti. They've asked for my help."

Diane looked crestfallen. "Chris, at some point you have to provide for yourself, for your future." She touched his arm when she said 'future' hoping that he would connect her with his future.

"You could come with me."

"Chris. Back home I'm halfway along the partnership fast-track. I can't just drop everything and..."

He turned to her and Diane felt her knees begin to melt. His brown eyes, his sincere eyes, his penetrating eyes seemed to caress her very soul. His strength, physical and spiritual wrapped her in safety and security. All the regrets she had in not pursuing a relationship with him in the past flooded back into her heart.

"I can't just drop everything," she repeated.

"Your things. Do you own them or do they own you?"

"Chris! That's not *fair*. It's not just things. It's accomplishment. Past and future. I *help* people."

"Diane. You're a good person. But who chooses who you help?"

"The partners choose. But if I make partner—"

"You'll be part of the firm. And the firm has bills to pay."

"Chris. Do you even have ten dollars saved for your

76

retirement?"

"I have a small retirement savings plan. Ten thousand dollars. You?"

Diane bit her lip. Her own plan was thirty times the size of his. "Chris, ten thousand won't last you even a year."

"The people in Haiti. They have less."

"Chris."

He shrugged. The two Jamaican lawyers were typing into a tablet and passing it back and forth between them. Chris, sensing an imminent deal, walked over to stand close. Diane watched his eager face, remembering why she'd been so smitten with him, but also remembering why they had drifted apart.

The shuttle bus pulled to a gentle stop and Helen and Amanda, wearing bikinis, Save-the-Reef T-shirts, and sandals, jumped off the bus shouting, "Save the Reef, Save—". They stopped in mid-chant when they saw that no one else was there. The Canadian couple jumped onto the bus which swiftly pulled away.

Helen and Amanda strolled over to Chris and Diane, the only other two people wearing Save-the-Reef T-shirts. "What happened?" they asked in unison.

Diane pointed to the two Jamaican lawyers. "We may have a settlement. The lawyers are trying to firm up the deal."

Helen was suspicious. "What kind of deal?"

Diane looked the petite black woman up and down. Somehow she knew that Helen was a lesbian. Maybe it was the universe trying to tell her that since men weren't working out in her life she should try something different. She looked over at Chris who was chatting with Helen's tall, buxom and very, very blonde companion. The two were smiling and preening, occasionally touching. Chris glanced over at her. She blew him a kiss and pulled Helen away to explain the intricacies of the protections the proposed resolution would provide for the artificial reef.

Chris watched Diane slowly drift away. That was them. Always drifting apart. He returned his attention to Amanda. She could be just what he needed. One last fling before heading to Haiti. "What brought you to Jamaica?" he asked her.

Amanda bit her lip and turned away, suddenly looking like a

teenager. "Promise you won't laugh," she demanded.

"Cross my heart and hope to die." This was obviously not going to be an intellectual relationship. But what the hell, a fling required a meeting of bodies, not a meeting of minds. Out of the corner of his eye he saw the two Jamaican lawyers shake hands.

"I came here to determine my orientation," confessed Amanda.

"You mean whether you're gay?"

"Lesbian," she corrected.

"Do you like guys?" He removed his T-shirt and enjoyed the effect his happy smile, broad shoulders and rippling abs had on her.

Amanda gulped and nodded.

"Then you're not gay."

"I like girls too." She glanced at Helen who was flirting with Diane.

Chris followed her gaze and locked eyes with Diane. He raised an eyebrow. It was a small movement, barely a millimeter above his right eye. But Diane saw it and he saw that she saw it. He was asking whether they had a chance after all these years, he was saying that he wanted to give it a go.

Diane felt a deep yearning in her heart. But in her head she knew that any relationship with Chris was doomed. They were too different. Her wants and desires and plans contradicted his and vice versa. Being with Chris would be passionate and fun and life affirming. At first. Then there would be recriminations, each hating the other for frustrating the other's aspirations. She felt her heart shrink and fall into her belly. She shook her head and turned away so that he wouldn't see the tears welling in her eyes.

Chris saw Diane shake her head. He took a deep breath, but it didn't fill the emptiness in his heart. He returned his attention to Amanda. "Boys or girls, which do you like best?"

Amanda shrugged and shuffled her feet.

"Maybe this'll decide you." Chris picked her up by her waist and gently lifted her over his right shoulder, his hands holding her legs securely against the front of his body.

Helen watched Amanda being carried away. They blew kisses to each other. Diane looked back and forth between the two women, then led Helen towards the two Jamaican lawyers.

Amanda felt her breasts jiggle with every step Chris took. Her nipples pressed against the insides of her bikini top. He removed one of his hands to pat her bum and she felt herself warm deep inside her sex. She grabbed the back of his swim trunks to hold on. Now he wasn't just patting her bum, he was *squeezing* it! She felt his strides slow as he entered the water. One of his hands slid under her bikini bottom and dampness joined heat inside.

Chris could tell that Amanda worked out. All of her muscles were firm. But she was also flexible. And the muscles in her butt—her gorgeous round butt—were relaxed, soft. He carried her easily, enjoying her enjoying being carried.

Amanda held on as tightly as she could to his trunks to stop him from throwing her, back-first, into the water. But she needn't have worried, at least not on that count. He strode steadily, if ever more slowly, forward. She felt her feet dip into the water. Then her hands. His swim trunks became slippery in the salt water and they slipped free of her grasp. Chris' hands slid her down the front of his body, hugging her close, as he lowered her feet to the bottom.

When she was steady on her feet, Chris took her hands in his, pulled them beneath the water, and pressed them against the front of his swimsuit where his erection was pressing itself forward. "Do you like this?" he asked.

She nodded.

"Show me how much you like him."

Amanda gulped to hide her smile, then stroked him lightly through the swim trunks. He felt huge!

"Maybe my swimsuit is getting in the way," he mused.

Amanda gingerly lifted his trunks up and out over his erection. He *was* huge! He pressed his legs together and his trunks slid down to the ocean floor. She stroked him some more, her pussy yearning to have him inside.

His hands undid the knot on her string bikini, leaving it hanging loosely on her shoulders. One hand caressed each breast and she felt her nipples poking up against his palms. She closed her eyes to savor every ridge in his hands. Chris' fingers found her hot little buds, lightly squeezing them between thumb and forefinger, sending jolts through her arms and into the fingers which were holding him, tenderly stroking him.

Chris gently twisted his thumb and forefinger around her nipples. Amanda's knees turned to jelly. She tried to maintain her balance but she was falling backwards. She held on— He yelped and grabbed her wrists. Her eyes jerked open and she let go of him.

"Sorry," she apologized.

"It's okay," he said, touching himself to make sure. "Just remember, it's not a handle."

"Sorry," she repeated.

"Maybe we should finish this ashore."

Amanda nodded and, as soon as they'd readjusted their swimwear, they walked, hand in hand, out of the water.

There was no one left on the beach. No demonstrators. No Jamaican lawyers. No policemen. The construction workers would be back tomorrow. But today, the construction site had been abandoned. Chris popped around a corner, came back with a bag, and led Amanda around piles of debris, piles of gravel and half-dug foundation pillars. Finally, in the midst of all this desolation was a coconut tree and a small lawn.

Chris opened his bag, took out a blanket and laid it on the lawn. He dipped to one knee and swept his hand across the blanket at an attempt at gallantry. Amanda giggled, curtsied and plopped her bottom in the middle of the blanket.

Chris removed his swim trunks and stepped forward to stand in front of Amanda. She reached upward to gingerly touch him. Even half flaccid, he was still *huge*. Her attention quickly returned him to full readiness.

Chris watched her hands. The woman sitting on the blanket in front of him was full bodied and fit. Making love to her would be a treat to savor for many months to come.

"Do you want him?" he asked.

Her answer was to kiss his erection, and he twitched. She jerked her head back.

"Don't worry, he won't bite," Chris assured her.

This time, she took the head of his penis into her mouth. He groaned. She tried for more, but all she could accommodate was three inches.

"Don't worry, use your hands," he encouraged.

She stroked him up and down, twirling her tongue around what she'd managed to take into her mouth. He groaned again. Was he being kind or was he really enjoying her feeble efforts?

He dipped his knees and popped himself out of her mouth.

"Women can suck," he told her. "Women can touch, women can fondle. But there's one thing no woman can ever do for you."

He pulled her to her feet and kissed her full on her mouth. She broke free of his kiss as he pulled her bikini top away.

"Women can kiss too," she reminded him.

He reached forward, undid the strings on each side of her bikini bottom and let it slide to the blanket. He lifted her up, his hands on her thighs just below her buttocks, her pubic hairs pressed against his stomach. Amanda's feet were far from the ground and there was only air behind her spine, but he held her so firmly she felt completely safe. "Has any woman ever done this for you?" he asked.

Amanda's response was a kiss full on his mouth, her tongue invading the inner recesses between his teeth. He enjoyed the kiss, and joined in her tongue-play. But when his hands showed no indication of lowering her, she broke off the kiss.

"Has any woman ever done this for you?" he repeated.

"No."

He lowered her an inch and she felt a frisson tug at her sex. "Or this?"

"No."

He lowered her again. His penis wasn't touching her, but she could feel its heat. "Or this?"

"No. Please!"

"Please what?"

"Please, just, *please*!" He lowered her again and she could feel him touching her. "Please!" she cried.

"Has any woman ever made you beg like this?"

"No! Please!"

"Please what? Tell me exactly what you want me to do."

"Put yourself inside." He lowered her and she felt his tip slide inside, but no further than she'd been able to accommodate in her mouth. Still, he was *big*, and she gasped.

"Is that what you want?"

"Yes! More." He dropped her a few more inches. He began to fill her, to stimulate her sexually, to make her feel wanted. "Further! All the way."

Slowly, inexorably, he lowered her, inch by inch, over every ridge of his cock. She bit her lip to banish the discomfort. But then their pubic bones touched and she was filled, fulfilled.

"Has any woman ever done this for you?" he demanded.

"No," she gasped.

She was tight, wonderfully tight. And when she squeezed him he knew that she would be putty in his hands. He started to lift her back up.

"No, I want," she protested.

"You want what?" he mocked. "Say it. And use the proper word."

"Fuck." It was the softest of soft whispers.

"Fuck what?" he asked, matching her whisper.

"Fuck *me*," begged Amanda, still whispering.

Chris lifted her all the way off his shaft and gently laid her on the blanket in front of him. Her pussy was swollen and pink. His cock swayed, master of worlds. He knelt down between her legs and slowly, with infinite gentleness, reinserted himself into her. This time her muscles knew what to expect and it was easier. He began to slowly rock his hips, pulling himself out, pushing himself back in.

"Has any woman ever done this for you?" he demanded.

"No!" she wailed.

No woman had ever lifted her over her shoulder and carried her into the ocean. No women had ever lifted her up and slowly lowered her into sexual congress. No woman had ever filled her the way he was filling her. No woman had ever mastered her body with physical strength. No woman had ever stared into her eyes while fucking her— fucking her with cock, fucking her with eyes, fucking her *mind*. And no woman had ever stoked such a white-hot arousal inside her loins!

Amanda's insides turned to liquid then jolted rock hard, melting, then solidifying in waves, wave after wave, which wracked up and down her body, threatening to break it into little pieces. Then the waves softened, massaging pleasure into her every cell, lifting her up to float atop mother ocean, lifting her up to the warmth of the sun.

No woman had ever done *that* for Amanda. Nor had any woman ever given up her life-force for her, thought Amanda as she felt his gently flow down her thighs.

Chapter 9

Saturday began grey and then turned wet with rain. The rain was constant, sometimes heavy but never less than a drizzle. Usually the main dining area would clear out after meals, but now it remained mostly full since it was the only place available for guests to socialize with each other. Chatting groups ranged in size from two to twenty.

Staff circulated in case any of the guests needed anything. But the resort staff studiously refrained from pointing out the obvious ecological fact that rain was an essential component of the *rain*forest. They had learned the hard way that guests did not appreciate having this pointed out to them.

Damini Agarwal was in a corner chatting with Amanda Waterman whose blonde hair and only slightly tanned skin contrasted delightfully with the dark skin of the South East Asian woman.

"It's too bad about you and Bassim," commiserated Amanda.

"Thank you," replied Damini. "But it was likely going to happen at some point, so better now than later."

"But you said he was becoming more adventurous?"

"Only in the most minimal of ways. Now that he's gone, I have to face up to the fact that I was deceiving myself."

"What are you going to do now?"

She knew that Amanda was asking about what she'd do when she returned home, alone, to her house, to her real estate agency. But Damini's concerns were more here and now and she kept a close eye on Claire and Eric who were part of a six-person group on the other side of the room. "I don't know," was all she said.

The other two couples in the group—Nathan and Sophie Weiland and Charles and Carmen Johnson divided their attention between watching the rain and listening to Eric and Claire's recriminations.

"And I suppose you're going to tell me that she was the only one?" Claire accused in a high-pitched whine.

"It's the truth," responded Eric.

"Why her?"

"She was available."

"*I* was available."

"Sure, in between running and preparing to run and resting from running. Sure, you were available."

"You like running."

"Only because it's the only way to be with you."

There was a moment of tenderness between the warring couple. Carmen waited for the moment to peak and begin to fade before she spoke. "You need to decide what Eric's infidelity means."

Claire's eyes shot daggers at the veteran swinger. "It *means* that he's a cheating asshole."

Carmen was unfazed. "That's one of the meanings you can choose."

"What other meaning is there?"

"You, both of you, can choose to have it be a point of forgiveness, a point to move forward from. You can choose to see it as a symptom of problems within your marriage."

"You can choose," piped in Nathan, "to either reinvigorate your marriage or to let it wither and die."

"I had sex with her husband," confessed Claire.

"And how did that make you feel?" probed Carmen.

"Empty."

Carmen turned to Eric. "And how did it feel when you had sex with Damini?"

Eric could see the South East Asian beauty out of the corner of his eye. It took all of his willpower to keep from looking directly at her. "Empty," he answered. That was a lie. Sex with Damini had been exciting and invigorating. But now was not the time for historical truth, now was the time to build a *new* truth with his wife.

"And how does it feel when you have sex with Claire?"

"Safe and secure. It feels like I'm home."

No wonder he stepped out, thought Charles.

But Carmen wasn't ready to give up. She turned to Claire: "And how do you feel when you run?"

Claire's eyes lit up, but she wasn't sure she'd heard right. "When I *run*?"

Carmen nodded.

"I feel exhilarated and alive!"

"And when you have sex?"

"Like Eric said, safe and secure. Home."

"Safe and secure," noted Nathan, "Home. All of that is fine. But shouldn't sex be more than just safe and secure? Hasn't it ever been *exciting*?"

Claire thought back to their honeymoon. Eric thought back to his last hotel-room tryst with Damini. Both nodded.

"If you want to have a marriage, a real marriage," continued Nathan, "you both have to decide that that's what you want. You have to decide what that means, the sacrifices you must each make, the rules you must each follow. But most of all, you have to heal, you have to nurture each other."

Everyone nodded. Sophie looked at Nathan with admiration.

"And you have to have fun!" added Charles.

Eric and Claire looked at each other, agreeing.

The others clapped. Eric and Claire blushed.

Nathan nudged Claire. "The first step is forgiveness."

Claire waved Damini to come over and join them. Damini was uncertain. Nathan and Sophie waved her over. Damini looked at Amanda who nodded. Damini rose, trepidation pounding in her heart, and walked over to Nathan, keeping the older man between herself and Claire. Amanda sat behind Damini.

Nathan angled his head towards Claire.

The blue-eyed woman took a deep breath. "I'm sorry," she said.

Damini didn't know what to make of that. "I'm the one who should be sorry."

Claire rose, kissed Damini on the top of her head. She and Eric left the group, walking hand in hand. Helen and Diane, ebony and ivory, strolled in and joined the group.

"So, what's your favorite Hedo story?" asked Charles.

Sophie smiled. "The first time we came, late eighties, we had no idea about the theme nights. We had to raid the gift shop, run into town to try to cobble outfits together."

"What about pajama night?"

She shook her head. "We had flannel outfits, covered us from head to toe."

Everyone laughed at that.

"What about you?" asked Sophie.

Charles looked at Carmen, then back at Sophie. "The first time we came to Hedo, we'd heard about swinging, but we'd never experienced it. There was a group of swingers in the disco. We ended up in the thick of it. Hands groping everywhere. Couples having sex on the stage—right out in the open! I creamed my shorts, right on the dance floor."

Sophie turned to Carmen. "What did *you* think of that?"

"I was shocked!" She shared a chuckle with Charles. "But then it was *so* much fun! We went back to the room, cleaned Charles up, then came back for more."

"And all this was okay with resort management?" asked Helen.

Carmen smiled and moved her head back and forth. "They tried to keep a lid on the more boisterous of the couples. But I only heard of one couple being asked to leave."

"And that was after their third warning," Charles chimed in.

"It didn't help that they were lesbians," noted Carmen. Charles nodded agreement.

"I thought that Hedonism was LGBT friendly?" queried Helen.

Charles extended his hand out, flat, palm facing down and rocked his hand. "Yes and no. The swingers love lesbians, especially the ones available for threesomes. Gay guys not so much. The resort was pretty cool back then. But they had to make a show of not letting the debauchery get out of hand. Public sex was illegal in Jamaica and some politicians were suggesting that Hedo be closed."

"What about now?" probed Helen.

"Similar. Public sex is still illegal." He looked around the group, seemed to detect a consensus, and continued, "They're probably a little more strict," said Charles with Carmen, Sophie and Nathan nodding agreement. "The disco has never been the same."

"What about the hot tub?" asked Helen.

Sophie smiled. "You can get away with a lot under water."

"Speaking of water," interjected Charles, "has anyone been out to scuba this week?"

Diane nodded. "Once. Saw two Leopard Rays."

"How much does scuba cost?" Helen wanted to know.

"It's included," said Charles. "Even the lessons. Everything's all-inclusive at Hedo."

"Except the spa," noted Sophie. "You have to pay if you want a massage."

The rain seemed to be letting up and the group dispersed. Carmen and Charles made it to the seaside grill, which was empty, before the deluge started to drench the resort once more.

"What do you think?" she asked.

Charles thought about that, mostly trying to guess what his wife was referring to. The ocean was barely visible through the rain. He had time. But after a few moments, he gave up. "About what?" he asked.

"Swinging."

A wide topic. He decided on a vague answer. "It's fun." He had no idea where the conversation was going.

"But is it building our marriage or tearing it down?"

"I love you, Carmen." He decided to play it safe while drawing her out. Besides, it was true, he did love her.

"I'm serious."

"So am I." Where the hell was this going?!?

"Maybe we should stop swinging, keep what we have just between the two of us?"

"We could tone it down," he allowed.

"Especially back home."

He nodded. "Keep it just a vacation thing?"

She nodded and smiled. He felt the knot in his stomach slowly unwind. Once again he'd made the right guesses.

"Maybe explore kinky sex in the basement?" he ventured.

She punched his shoulder and smiled. They held hands and stared out into the rain. It was coming straight down, each large drop making a depression in the sand.

By dinnertime, the storm had passed and Charles and Carmen made their way to the dining room, dressed in accord with the evening's theme: hats and heels. He wore a top hat, patent leather wing-tips and a little black bikini. A walking stick lent an aura of elegance. She wore a wide-brimmed hat with a long feather extending halfway down her back, skimpy bikini and stiletto heels, all pink.

They spotted Amanda sitting alone. Charles nudged his wife in Amanda's direction, "One last fling before heading home?"

She pinched his nipple. "Sure!" Then she marched over to Amanda and asked if they could sit at her table. When she responded in the affirmative, they sat down on either side of her.

After dinner, Charles ordered brandies for the trio. "Have you been to the Romping Room?" he asked Amanda.

She shook her head. "What's a romping room?"

"It's a special room where anything goes."

"Anything?"

He couldn't tell what she was thinking, but he nodded and smiled.

"Sounds like fun!"

Charles and Carmen each kissed a cheek.

In the romping room, Charles led them to a small room just to the left of the entrance. On one wall was an enclosed shower. The other wall was deep purple velour. There were several mattresses. At the far end was a bench with a large mirror behind it. Two couples sat on the bench, as if waiting for the show to begin.

Charles directed Amanda's attention just slightly to the left. There were chains hanging from the ceiling, a makeshift cage, a sawhorse-like contraption and an X-shaped cross. "Have you ever tried bondage?" he asked her.

She shook her head.

Carmen gave Amanda a light swat to her bum and knelt on the sawhorse. "Me first!" she proclaimed.

Amanda had no idea what was going on. Charles gave her a light hug. "Make her say whatever you want. Touch her, pinch her, tickle her, spank her until she submits."

Amanda softly spanked Carmen's right buttock. Her bikini barely covered anything, so the sound was loud in the small room. "Say 'I will obey you'," the blonde amazon demanded.

"Never!" came Carmen's muffled response.

Amanda spanked her twice more, once on each buttock. Carmen remained silent.

Charles removed his wife's stilettos and hit her buttocks with the heels.

"Ow!" protested Carmen.

"Say it," demanded Amanda.

"It."

Amanda swatted her insolent knave, harder this time. "Say 'I will obey you'," she specified.

"Never!"

Charles motioned towards his wife's breasts. "Pinch her nipples."

Amanda reached around to pinch Carmen's nipples. Her large breasts felt slightly odd, and there was a scar. But the nipples were thoroughly aroused. She took each nipple between thumb and forefinger. "Say 'I will obey you'," she commanded.

Carmen remained defiantly silent. Amanda twisted until Carmen gasped. "Say it," she demanded.

"Never!"

Amanda didn't dare twist harder and let go of Carmen's nipples.

"Slap her pussy," encouraged Charles.

"Don't you dare," hissed Carmen.

Amanda hesitated.

"Like this." Charles demonstrated, but he barely touched his wife's bikini.

"Charlie, you bastard!" yelped Carmen.

Charles tapped his wife's bikini again, again barely touching it. To Amanda he said, "But harder. Touch her to make sure you have the right spot, then let her have it."

Amanda reached between Carmen's legs. She was warm and damp. Nothing artificial there! Amanda pulled her hand back.

"I will obey you! I will obey you!" shouted Carmen, doing her best to move her rump out of the way. Amanda helped her slave up.

"My turn next," proclaimed Charles, positioning himself against the X-shaped cross. Carmen tied off his wrists and ankles with Velcro straps, then pulled his bikini down to reveal a very, very full erection.

Carmen pinched his nipples and twisted, almost yanking them off. "That's what you told your bitch to do, didn't you?"

"Yes, Mistress," he gasped.

She swatted his balls. "And this?"

"Yes, Mistress, I'm sorry Mistress."

Carmen turned to Amanda. "What should we do with him?" she asked.

"Is he ticklish?"

"No," he wailed. "Carmen! Please!"

Carmen smiled evilly. "Yes, our slave is ticklish. But only in two very special spots."

"Where?" asked Amanda.

Carmen started to speak then stopped. She shook her head. Charles looked relieved.

Carmen stood on her tiptoes and kissed Amanda. "If I tell you, will you relieve me of my vow to obey you?"

Amanda nodded.

"And will you do whatever I say?"

Amanda nodded again, "Yes, Mistress."

Carmen moved around behind the cross.

"No, Carmen! Please!" wailed Charles.

Carmen ignored his pleas and motioned towards his crotch. "Grab his cock. Grab his balls. And watch where I put my fingers."

Charles balls did their best to shrink themselves into the space between his thighs, but Amanda had no trouble holding onto his cock. Carmen's fingertips moved into the middle of his armpits.

"Carmen. Please," he blubbered.

When her fingertips touched the back of his armpits, he twitched. It wasn't much, he was trying to hold himself still, but Amanda felt it in her hands. Carmen stroked up and this time the twitch was unmistakable, jerking Charles from side to side. Carmen stroked her fingers down and this time Charles' cock thrust forward as his torso bent backwards.

Carmen removed her fingers and he sucked oxygen into his lungs. "You bitch," Charles wheezed as his wife came back around in front.

Carmen replaced Amanda's hands with her own on his gonads. "Your turn," she told Amanda.

It took Amanda a little longer than it had taken Carmen, but soon she had Charles writhing and thrashing just like his wife had. When she sensed he'd had enough, she lifted her hands off him.

"Don't stop," Carmen told her.

"Carmen, please," he pleaded.

"And if you come, I'll cut it off."

"Carmen—"

But his plea was terminated by Amanda's fingers on his tickle spots. He writhed in mock agony, struggling against the spasms wracking his body and his wife's efforts to complete her hand job.

Mercifully, Amanda withdrew her fingers and freed Charles' wrists. "What's next?" she asked.

Carmen looked disappointed that the tickle session was ending. She pointed to the mattress next to the X-shaped cross. "Remove your clothes. Then kneel and grab the chains."

Amanda removed her clothes and they admired her beauty: tall and blonde, with all the curves God had intended. But Amanda remained standing. "And then what?" she asked.

Carmen smiled. "And then you're going to lick and kiss me. And then you're going to lick and kiss Charles. And then we're going to fuck you. And then you're going to finish licking me."

Amanda nodded, knelt, and reached up the chains, pulling her full breasts up and proud.

Carmen lifted her crotch to Amanda's mouth. The odor was pungent and powerful. But the angle was wrong and Amanda could only flick her tongue against a small part of Carmen's sex. She had more luck with Charles' cock and managed to suck its tip into her mouth.

Then Charles knelt down in front of her, rolled a condom over his cock and inserted it inside her. He wasn't as big as Chris. She tried to shut her legs, but Carmen slapped lightly back and forth against her thighs.

"Be still," Carmen told her, a voice from behind.

Amanda felt Carmen's fingers press upwards, not forward, but against her ass. The fingers withdrew, leaving her alone with Charles' cock. But Carmen's fingers came back wet and slick. Two fingers slid inside Amanda's back door and she was suddenly fuller than full.

"Now you can shut your legs."

Amanda clamped her legs together. Charles was pumping in and out. Carmen started to match his thrusts, but she pulled out when he pushed in. Amanda's legs were jelly. If her hands hadn't been in white-knuckle grip around the chains, she would have collapsed onto the mattress.

"Are you ready?" asked Charles.

Amanda wasn't, then she was. She nodded.

"Then scream!"

"Fuck!" screamed Amanda. She felt her ass clench around Carmen's fingers. Spasm after spasm shot upwards from the fingers, up her spine and into her neck, each one higher than the last. Finally one exploded inside her skull. But thankfully the spasms had weakened by that point and Amanda was able to maintain consciousness. Barely! She heaved air into her lungs as the next spasm wracked up her spine. Then the waves became gentle and she stared to float.

Charles had never felt such strength envelope his cock. Amanda's flush spread heat up his belly and into his chest. She squeezed, forcing him to pump every last drop into her, then she milked even more out of him. Powerful pleasure gripped his entire midsection.

Amanda felt her fingers being pried off the chain and her body being laid down on the mattress. Charles kept her thighs pressed against each other as he unrolled the condom from around his cock. There was something sticky there.

Carmen laid down behind Amanda and kissed her cheek. "Are you ready to finish me?"

Amanda nodded. They rolled her onto her side and Carmen kissed down her body, raising her leg to give Amanda full access to her sex. Charles had moved around behind his wife and Amanda was aware of him pleasuring his wife's backside. Carmen's pussy was bubbly oysters. Amanda lapped the froth and licked up and down Carmen's slit, circling her clit at the top of each stroke. She slid a finger inside and managed to elicit a low groan.

Carmen's legs jerked. Then Amanda felt little spasms on her fingers. One large spasm, then several smaller clenches. Carmen groaned the end of her orgasm. The trio hugged themselves together and drifted off to sleep, their bodies spent, their bodies awash in warmth and pleasure.

Chapter 10

All good things (and thankfully all bad things, though this is rarely pointed out) must come to an end. And today it fell upon Rosie to check several of the departing guests out of the resort. As luck would have it, the weather was sunny and hot.

Keiko and Yoshi, the young Japanese couple who had been slated to spend a sedate sojourn at Sandals, but who had instead spent a sultry week at Hedo, were the first to be directed into the shuttle which would take them to the airport. As they handed their keycard over, they kissed. "What happens at Hedo," he began.

"Stays at Hedo," she finished.

Damini remained silent through the process of completing the paperwork and paying for her spa visit. Alternating waves of emotion: sadness, relief, joy and excitement filled her lungs. Dominating all these was a feeling of anticipation for the future. Freedom was frightening and exhilarating all at the same time.

Amanda lounged on a couch at the far end of the entrance foyer. Her shuttle wouldn't leave until later that afternoon. She didn't want the gut-wrench of goodbyes, but she did want to watch the departure of those with whom she'd shared so much during the past week.

There were Carmen and Charles, a bit wobbly on their feet. Amanda smiled at the memory of her own contribution to their wobbliness. Tomorrow they would be back at their government jobs, dreaming of their next trip to Jamaica.

Next was Chris, backpack slung over his left shoulder, radiating power and glory and masculinity. She felt a stirring deep in her loins. Why was he going to Haiti? Why couldn't he come back with her, to her gym. They could—

And then he was gone. Gone forever. If only she could rush after him, if only… She half lifted herself from the couch, then slouched back down. She was being foolish. If not now, when? Now was the time to be foolish. She jumped to her feet and raced forward. But the shuttle pulled away. And Chris was gone, gone forever.

As Amanda settled back into the couch, Helen and Diane, holding hands, dressed to the nines, rolled their luggage into the lobby. Lawyer and consultant, power couple for the ages. Amanda wondered whether she should have made a play for them, or at least one of them.

They were talking about a penthouse condo, high above the lake, plans to take the city by storm. Amanda shook her head, too rich for her blood.

Besides, she had come to the realization that she liked men. Women were fine, but as an appetizer, not as a main dish. Men, for all their faults and frailties and foibles, were where the action was. Certainly, of all the people leaving that morning it was Chris, and only Chris, who had stirred any reaction in her. She rose and went back to her room to pack.

Diane and Helen weren't taking the two-hour shuttle to the airport. Instead, they had booked a ten-minute flight in one of Tim Air's single-engine propeller planes. A two-minute taxi ride whisked to the Negril Airport. 'Airport' was generous; in reality it was just a long strip of tarmac.

As the tiny plane banked over Hedonism, they looked down and remembered the night before. They had played a gambling game that had revolved around a particularly violent action-adventure movie, making bets based on what would come next: who would be killed, in which quadrant the next weapon would appear, whether the love scene would feature nipples or butts. Each loss required the removal of a piece of clothing, the downing of a shot of alcohol, the singing of a song, or the performance of a sexual act.

Helen, her black skin bare except for three spots of white, had misjudged the next gangster to die and performed a striptease with her white bra, leaving only a white satin thong protecting her modesty. At Diane's insistence, she played with her nipples until they pointed proudly away from her breasts. At the next sex scene, Diane guessed butts but it was a nipple which had first appeared and she had to let Helen suck on her own nipples through her lacy bra before removing it. Now all that protected the brunette's modesty was a lacy black thong.

The movie ended without further bets being won or lost which meant that Helen lost once again.

"I want to see you touch yourself," demanded Diane. "I want to see your panty pressed into your slit. I want to see a righteous camel toe."

Helen complied, feeling the tingles of arousal from her finger, feeling the tingles of the revenge she was plotting. After a few moments, Diane bent in for a better look and Helen pulled her face into her crotch, right into the center of the camel toe she'd so carefully manufactured.

When she released the white woman, Helen asked her, "Are you ready for toys?"

Diane was immediately wary. She would have been even more wary, but several shots of rum had dampened her inhibitions. "I didn't bring any toys," she said.

Helen reached into her drawer and brought out a double-ended dildo. It was pink silicone, each end shaped like a penis. "I tried to find something that didn't look like a cock, but they're all like this," she apologized.

Diane kissed her. "As long as it works."

They each slipped their thongs off. Now Diane was totally white, Helen totally black. Except inside where they were both pink.

Helen took one end of the dildo and sucked it into her mouth. Then she handed it to Diane, holding her finger to mark how far she'd sucked it into her mouth. "Think you can suck if further?"

Diane sucked in at least an inch more than Helen had, but before she could remove it from her mouth, Helen sucked the other end into her own mouth. The two women's faces inched closer and closer as each tried to outdo the other. But, try as they might, there was still six inches separating them.

Helen pulled the dildo out of her own mouth, then out of Diane's. She leaned back on the bed and carefully inserted the dildo as far as it would go into her vagina. She wagged the other end back and forth. Diane slid her right leg under Helen's left, the dildo into her own vagina and angled her left leg over Helen's right leg.

Diane slid the dildo ever deeper and finally her pussy was touching Helen's. The two women reached over and grabbed the other's upper hip to hold themselves together, feeling the dildo fill them, adjusting its thrusts to brush against their most sensitive spots. They began to rock back and forth, each enjoying the sensations of the other's pussy lips fluttering along her own. Then as they gained confidence, they held each other tighter and rocked harder.

This had provoked their first orgasm, Helen first, then a few moments later Diane. They had lain together sweating.

Then Helen had asked, "Ready for round two?"

Diane had nodded. Helen had positioned Diane on all fours and then slid the dildo into her. Helen went on all fours, her butt facing Diane's, and slid the dildo partway into her own vagina.

But that hadn't been the end of Helen's play toy. She reached down between them and pressed hard against the center of the dildo. This had flipped a switch and the dildo had begun to vibrate.

"Yikes!" yelped Diane.

But before she'd had time for any further reaction, Helen pushed back, slapping her butt against Diane's. The dildo in place, they had slapped against each other's butts until their second, and more powerful orgasm smacked them silly.

The vibrations in the dildo had been just like the vibrations which were now jiggling them inside the little plane on which they were flying high above Jamaica's north coast. Helen looked at Diane. Diane looked at Helen. The same memory coursed through their brains, through their loins. The two women didn't care how high off the ground they were. As far as they were concerned, they were about to join the mile-high club!

They stared straight ahead. They affected bored expressions. Their hands reached under skirts, under panties and found hot damp flesh. Their hands caressed hungrily against each other, urging the other to climax. Each glanced out the window urging the landscape below to slow its progress towards Montego Bay's international airport.

Each slid fingers inside the other, rocking them back and forth against the thumb pressed against each other's pubic bone. Helen came first, just a little gasp, but Diane felt the spasms against her fingers.

Diane let her own fingers slide out and Helen adjusted herself for a better angle. "Faster?" asked Diane.

The black woman nodded and Diane doubled the pace of her efforts under her lover's skirt.

Diane caught sight of the airport as the plane circled. "Faster?" she whispered and Helen nodded again. Diane increased her pace slightly, but she didn't dare go faster for fear of being too obvious. The runway was approaching. *The plane was less than a hundred feet above the ground.* Diane's fingers ached. Helen's breathing was shallow but Diane didn't know how close she was. The tarmac rushed up to the plane.

The wheels touched with a thud. Diane tried to pull her hand out but the jolt of the plane's landing pushed her fingers further inside Helen. Further, just far enough to stimulate just the right spot and Helen's orgasm gripped her fingers holding them in place. Helen gasped.

The plane was slowing to a stop. The pilot's head began to swivel. Helen's eyes were shut, little wheezes escaping her mouth

"The pilot's going to turn around!" Diane pleaded.

But Helen didn't care. She'd joined the mile-high club and she was going to feel every last tingle of her airborne orgasm.

"How was the flight," asked the pilot.

Diane was relieved to see Helen finally open her eyes. She was smiling from ear to ear.

Chapter 11

The day before, after the rest of the group had dispersed, Sophie and Nathan had remained in the dining room, watching the rain come down. The dull flat light had made them look even older than their sixty-plus years.

"Do you think we can follow our own advice?" she'd asked.

"To reinvigorate our marriage?"

She nodded. "To decide to sacrifice for each other, to heal, to nurture."

He reached for her hand and gave it a gentle squeeze. "Do you want to?"

She squeezed back and nodded. "But how do we..." Her voice trailed off at the gargantuan task. Every little disagreement had seemed to escalate. Past recriminations, some petty, some fundamental to their marriage, were dragged in to whose turn it was to empty the garbage. They often avoided talking for fear of stirring things up. The only time they shared emotional intimacy was when he accused her of never being willing to take the first step, or indeed any step, to repair the hurts they each inflicted on each other. Sex was good, they still enjoyed each other's company, but...

"There is a way," he ventured.

She turned to him, a faint glint of hope in her eyes. But she didn't smile for fear that this faint hope might be dashed.

"It's part of Japanese culture," he explained. "The Japanese had a small-village society. It was interdependent. It couldn't function if there was discord or rancor. So they developed ways of letting bygones be bygones, of forgiving the past, of moving forward."

Nathan turned so that they were each facing the other and took both her hands. "One of the methods they developed was the tea ceremony. The person seeking forgiveness performs the ceremony. The central moment is the pouring of the tea into the teacups. The ceremony itself celebrates the healing. The completion of the ceremony signals that the relationship has been repaired and restored to harmony."

Sophie had smiled at him and nodded.

The next day, Nathan woke at dawn and sat on the beach as the first rays of the sun began to dance across the water. It was time to compose a haiku, the peculiarly Japanese poem meant to convey pure emotion. Five syllables in the first line, seven in the second and five syllables in the final line.

His first line began, "Beautiful Negril". Then the second line "Sophie More Beautiful" was quickly replaced with "Trials and Tribulations". The poem concluded with "All Evaporate".

He looked at what he had scrawled. Possible, but perhaps he could do better. He began his next effort with "Wonderful sunrise" which swiftly became "Jamaican sunrise". The middle line was "Throw all life's cares and insults" which carried on to the finish "Into the sunset". Technically it got the 5/7/5 but it was too on the nose and the last two lines were really one line.

Nathan began again, striving for the imagery and emotion which were the epitome of Haiku verse. Roses. Cherry blossoms. Pain in the middle. Finish on an upbeat. After much scratching out and rewriting he finally had something satisfactory:

Rose petal blossom
Withering thorny insults
Into true beauty

When he returned to their room, Sophie was just beginning to stir. "Ready for breakfast?" he asked.

She grumbled and stomped to the bathroom while he checked his emails.

In the dining room, she was still waking up, so he took the opportunity to have one of the chefs prepare a custom omelet for him: ham, onion, green pepper. It was still steaming when he put the first bite into his mouth. Sophie was still working on a small bowl of yogurt.

After breakfast, they scoured the resort for what they'd need for the tea ceremony. The Japanese restaurant—Harrysan—furnished them with powdered green tea and a teapot with a small candle underneath for reheating. Nathan would have preferred a larger pot from which he could scoop the tea in the traditional Japanese fashion, but such an item was apparently unavailable. The restaurant also supplied the small bowls which the Japanese used instead of the cups favored by Westerners. The main kitchen provided a small kettle for boiling the water and a spoon for scooping the tea. In the gift shop, they found marzipan sweets, a small parchment-colored notepad and a ribbon.

While returning to their room, he spotted something familiar on the ground and he guided them towards it.

But Sophie recognized it first. "Our stone!" she proclaimed.

Over the years, guests had painted their names on stones and left them around the resort. Now, many were elaborate pieces of art. But their stone was only their names and the year of their second visit to the resort. Nathan and Sophie read their names over and over again as they hugged their bodies together.

Back in their room, he placed the powdered green tea, sweets and the small bowls on plates and put the plates on the floor. When Sophie hadn't been looking, he had written out his haiku on the notepad, folded up the page into a tiny cube, and tied it with the ribbon. This he placed on the plate holding the marzipan sweets. He sat to the right of the plates, doing his best to find a comfortable position.

Sophie pointed to the parchment. "What's that?"

His only answer was a smile.

She sat on the floor opposite him and watched him prepare the tea. Preparing the tea, setting the stage for the ritual, was integral to the ceremony and he felt honored by her rapt attention to his actions.

When the water boiled, Nathan carefully scooped green tea powder into the teapot. He unplugged the kettle, waited for the water to stop bubbling, and carefully stirred water into the teapot. He added just enough water for the tea to be easily poured, but not so much as to make it watery. His movements were elegant, precise.

Nathan took a deep breath and looked into his wife's eyes. All their joys, all their arguments swirled between them. Soon only the former would remain.

He reached for the teapot but Sophie extended her hand towards its handle. "Would it be alright if I poured?" she asked.

Nathan looked deep into his wife's eyes and saw that she understood the significance of her request. She too was seeking reconciliation, was seeking forgiveness for her part in their troubles. They each took a breath.

He nodded and withdrew his hand. She lifted the teapot with a gentle sweeping motion and centered the spout in the exact center of the first of the two small bowls. Her pour was accurate, no splash, not a drop spilled. She set the teapot down. Her elegant movements had brought honor to their household. He couldn't tell for sure, her movements were so soft, so refined, but she seemed to bow. Sophie lifted the full bowl between two fingers from each hand and proffered it to him. He slid his fingers under hers and accepted her offering. They smiled at each other.

He held his bowl in mid-air, at the exact point where the transfer had been made, while he watched her careful movements as she poured tea into her own bowl. When she lifted her bowl up, they bowed their mutual respect.

The tea was *bitter*! They quickly set their bowls down and each furiously unwrapped one of the sweets and took large bites. So this is why sweets were part of the traditional ceremony! Afterwards, they sipped the tea and nibbled on the sweets, relaxing into the glow of the ceremony.

Nathan reached down and picked up the parchment cube. Sophie watched the delicacy of his movements with a mixture of fascination and impatience. What was inside?!? Nathan carefully unfolded each edge until the page was flat in front of him. He took a deep breath, but when he spoke, his voice was soft:

Rose petal blossom
Withering thorny insults
Into true beauty

Sophie felt a tear trickle down her cheek. The poem was so wonderful. The moment was so wonderful. Her husband was so *wonderful*! She reached out for the page and he gave it to her. She opened it and read the poem to herself. She tried but could not remember any thorny insults. A tear landed on the bottom corner of the parchment.

"I love you," she told him.

"I love you too."

"I love all your virtues."

He nodded a reciprocal vow.

"I love all your faults," she told him.

"You have only virtues."

"Nathan."

He took a deep breath. "I love your fault."

"Nathan!" She swatted his leg and bit back a smile.

"Alright. Both of them."

"Nathan!" This time she couldn't hide her smile.

He smiled back. "I love your faults."

"I promise to always share my thoughts and feelings."

"I promise to share."

They reached out and squeezed each other's hands, then stood, trying to coax sensation back into their lower limbs.

"Shall we go for a walk and admire the sunset?"

Dinner was chicken from the nude-beach grill, French fries and ketchup. Food had never tasted so good. The bottom of the sun kissed the ocean, then caressed her as he slid beneath. His rays danced in the heavens.

Back in their room, Sophie knew that Nathan would try to please her physically. But she also knew that it had been a long and very emotional day. Sometimes he had difficulty achieving an erection, or maintaining it. Most of the time he had no difficulty—which was *outstanding* for a man in his sixties, especially after a long and eventful marriage—but every so often he hit a dry spell. She didn't mind; on those nights they cuddled. And she'd discouraged him from investigating ED drugs; she wanted their sex, or the lack of it, to be natural.

But Sophie needn't have worried. As soon as Nathan removed his towel, she saw that he was ready for action. She felt a stirring inside her sex. A flaccid penis did nothing for her no matter how large it was, but one fully erect, *especially* one fully erect just for her, that was a different story!

She dropped her own towel and felt her husband's eyes roam across her naked flesh. He paused at her breasts and at her crotch—he was a *man* after all, but his eyes also lingered on her hips, her legs and her shoulders. She knew she wasn't as alluring as she'd been on their wedding night, but it was still nice that he thought her attractive. She felt warmth spread throughout her body and dampness gather below.

Nathan led her to the king-size bed and laid her down atop the soft cotton sheets. They smiled at each other as he adjusted himself between her legs. She felt him press against her sex, gently but firmly. Sometimes she had to reach below to guide him, but tonight all she had to do was to rock her hips a smidgen and he slid right in.

Nathan exhaled a momentarily relief. His worst fear was always to lose his erection as he tried to find the right spot to slide in. It hadn't happened often, but often enough that it was always in the back of his mind. But now that he was sliding in and still strong and virile, there would be no worries—he could relax and *enjoy*.

It always felt good to be filled, to be taken and tonight was no different. She locked eyes with her husband and they gloried in the moment when their public bones touched. Then he pressed hard against her and rotated, sending little frissons up her spine. He pulled back out and began long strokes, each stroke stoking the fires within her sex.

It might have been an old married couple in the missionary position—the most vanilla of vanilla sex—but with a mirror in the ceiling, even vanilla had spice. Sophie watched her husband's glutes clench inward as he plunged himself insider her, then flatten as he withdrew. Over and over again, she never tired of watching the sight and feeling what it meant down below. His back arched. His leg muscles twitched.

Nathan knew she was watching his butt and he waited patiently until her eyes were back on his once more. There it was: the flash of recognition! Her eyes were looking up into his. He knew she'd want to look away, to look up at his butt in the mirror, but he locked onto her eyes and she was his.

Sophie felt warmth suffuse her heart, then spread throughout her entire body. The young ones might glory in intense, even fierce, orgasms centered on their sexual organs. But this climax, warmth in every cell of her being was by far the most satisfying and fulfilling.

He felt her eyes melt as they conceded his power over her, he felt her sex twitch around his cock, he felt his heart soar with his power over her. But it was a benign power and he would use it only to pleasure her, to pleasure his Sophie. He stroked in and out, wet friction all the way to heaven.

She couldn't move her eyes. She couldn't move her body. She didn't struggle; she gave herself willingly. And then she felt it, felt him being overwhelmed. She knew he was on the cusp of climax, knew it even before he did. She wanted to look at his butt, but even more, she wanted to look deep into his eyes as he surrendered his soul to her, as he felt her surrender her soul to him.

The End.

BACK NOTES

Thank you for reading this story. If you enjoyed it, please take a moment to post a review.

For my most recent publications, please see my author profile

Stories featuring Mistress Megan:
Pro Dom Her First Client
Pro Dom 2 Hugo
Pro Dom 3 Cross Dresser
Pro Dom 4 Hugo & Sheila (upcoming)
Pro Dom 5 Cold (upcoming)
Pro Dom 6 Lucas Visits Again (upcoming)
Pro Dom 7 Walk-in (upcoming)

Other Recent Stories

Tickle Test
Pay Back
Panty Play
Sponge Bath
Python Patty
You're So Sweet
Webcam Spank (imminent or already published)
Tiebreaker (imminent or already published)
Gunge Girl (upcoming)

The Lusty Lee Logs:
Prequel
The Case, Lusty Lee Log #1
Swinging, Lusty Lee Log #2
Strip Club, Lusty Lee Log #3
The Escort, Lusty Lee Log #4
Leather, Lusty Lee Log #5
Lusty Lee Box Set 1: All of the above!
Hedonism, Lusty Lee Log #6
Hedo II, Lusty Lee Log #7
Toronto, Lusty Lee Log #7a – bonus log
Cheaters, Lusty Lee Log #8
The Actor, Lusty Lee Log #9

Yearning, Lusty Lee Log #10
Lusty Lee Box Set 2: Logs 6 through 10 with bonus Log 7a
Scandal, Lusty Lee Log 11
Michael, Lusty Lee Log 12
Rum Balls, Lusty Lee Log 13
Massage, Lusty Lee Log 14
The Aide, Lusty Lee Log 15
Lusty Lee Box Set 3: Logs 11 through 15
Negotiator, Lusty Lee Log 16
Linebacker, Lusty Lee Log 17
Cosplay, Lusty Lee Log 18
Wrestling, Lusty Lee Log 19
Anger, Lusty Lee Log 20
Lusty Lee Box Set 4: Logs 16 through 20
Cops, Lusty Lee Log 21
Paintball, Lusty Lee Log 22
23 Interrogation
24 The Athlete
25 Sploshing
Lusty Lee Box Set 5: Logs 21 through 25
26 Choosing
27 Bondage
28 Tantra
29 Kundalini
30 Confronting
Lusty Lee Box Set 6: Logs 26 through 30 – the end

Please also consider reading other titles that I have authored as follows:

I Alien Vacation (novelette)

II Connie's Crop, a novel
Wherein mild-mannered Marsha pursuit of the magical whip pairs her with sexy Sheila and connects her with the darker side of sexuality.

III The Christopher Carter Series—already published

Carter's Chance II
 Private Party His
Private Party Hers
Private Party Box Set

Ryan's Reprieve
Cashmere Congress
Melissa's Moxie
Molly Madness
Melissa's Memories
Blackmail Bounce
Assisting Audrey
Splosh Scoundrel
Jody's Journal
Busted Bonds
Solicitor's Slip
Stakeout Story
Aural Artifact
 Mayan Magic
Party Photos
Buying Before
Cardiac Caress
Credit Card Con
Formatting Foam
Clinic Caper
Cosplay Clue
Witch's Wrath
 Carter's Climax Box Set: All 25 stories

And please check out my author profile at
https://www.smashwords.com/profile/view/JasonPinaster

For more adventurous versions of the covers, follow me on Pinterest:
https://www.pinterest.com/jasonpinaster/

Jason Pinaster

www.ingramcontent.com/pod-product-compliance
Lightning Source LLC
Chambersburg PA
CBHW031850170626
46807CB00004B/1663

* 9 7 8 1 3 7 0 0 5 3 3 4 6 *